Write of Passages

Writers' Ink

ISBN: 0968158242
ISBN-13: 978-0-9681582-4-1

"The privilege is not writing... it's to have someone read it. When you look at it that way, you realize the responsibility you have to put your very best on the page."

Javier A. Robayo

CONTENTS

Introduction

Every Tuesday evening, through all the seasons, a group of local storytellers gather at the old farmhouse at Sunnybrook Farm. We spend a couple of hours telling one another our stories – in prose or poetry. Some read tentatively because we are new to sharing our creations. Others are bold and confident, wanting critique to make the poem or story flow better, have more impact or create more compelling characters for the readers. Always, the goal of the group is to offer a chance for local writers to learn and improve our writing skills.

You may know some of us, maybe as a friend or neighbour or that young fellow who takes your ticket at the movie theatre. Some are accomplished authors with publishing credits to their name, others will never see their creations in print – except for between the covers of this assortment of short stories and poems we produced for your reading enjoyment. We intentionally did not choose a theme for this book. There are samplings of all kinds of prose and poetry - trips through memory land, some fantasy, some humour and some scary themes.

Publishing is one of the lessons for writers we decided to explore in producing this year's Anthology. Much effort has gone into making it happen. Most of our members have spent time in writing and editing submissions. It was a huge learning curve for most of us. We especially want to acknowledge the many days of work by Andy Lidstone, Lyle Meeres and John Burnham, who took on the heavy lifting on this project.

We welcome adult writers to join us. Check us out on our website or come to a meeting at the Sunnybrook Farm.

Enjoy!

Lauranne Hemmingway
President of Red Deer and Area Writers' Ink

Time to Write

By Carol Ritten Smith

Oh, glorious day. I'm all alone.
The family's away and nobody's home.
I've all day to write.

A fresh sheet of paper. Can't wait to start.
I write for an hour and pour out my heart.
Then sadly re-read it. It's bad. There's no doubt.
I crumple the paper and then throw it out.

Maybe a coffee will get words to flow—
A cookie or two and then watch me go.
So I write, then erase; I'm getting nowhere.
I'm grinding my teeth; I'm pulling my hair.
I'm blank as a slate; the words just won't come.
I've got a headache; am I really this dumb?
What? Lunchtime already? The morning's all spent.
I can't understand where all the time went.
I've wasted my day; my writing stinks.
I'm using up paper; I'm using up ink.
I ought to give up, try something else.
How 'bout a course to better myself?
Or find a new hobby, perhaps learn to knit.
Or speak a new language if time would permit.

Just put something down; I'm bound to get better.
Someday they'll say, "My, isn't she clever."
They'll know naught of the angst, nor of the tears,
Nor the hours, the days, the weeks, and the years
It took me to get on the best-sellers' rack.
Someday I'll be there, and I'll never look back.

So I scribble one word, then write a few more.
A simile here, a fun metaphor.
The words tumble out; I've hit my stride!
When suddenly a shout, as the door opens wide,
"Hi honey, we're back. We had a blast.
And how was your day?" he thinks to ask.
"Terrific," I say, though I'll never admit it:
I wrote the best stuff in the last fifteen minutes.

Colour

By Robert Swann

Close my eyes, look to the sun
The colour of life is the same as death
At the day's beginning and at its end
There is no black or white
Red is the colour of all and the gift of life

Colours

By Nicole Tarry

The world is not black and white; we are not black or white,
We have colours, we make colours, and we are colour.

It's easy to view these colours in nature,
The bright yellow of crops ready to be harvested,
The swirling blues of ocean next to sands of brown, tan, black and
sometimes pinks.
The standard forest greens, offset by vibrant shades of birds and
flowers.
The over bright and washed out colours of full direct sunlight,
The trees that darken with each passing cloud and approaching storm,
The shocking yellow and white of lightning as it strikes with fury.
The elusive technicolour that appears at the moment of sunset and
sunrise,
and eerie shades that emerge only in darkness and lit by moonlight.

But colours offer more than just what we see-
The hot colours of fire: red, yellow, orange and white
The icy cold tones of blue, purple and white,
The hurts of black, blue and purple bruises,
The deep metallic red of blood, life and death and
The rosy blush on skin made from a lover's caress.

Not only do we feel these colours physically but internally as well.
The happy yellow full of warmth and joy,
The queasy green of illness and nausea,
The fiery red of anger, ire and wrath,
The sorrow of blue, black and purple and
The orange of change and eclectic natures,
Not quite red and not quite yellow.

We take a stance and separate ourselves, depending on colours,
The arrays of green, brown, blue and grey of our eyes
The colours of hair white through red, brown, black, blond, and silver
The vastness of skin from light to dark and shades in between.

We go a step beyond to create bigger differences-
The pride of country as we gaze upon a flag,
The different shades denote value through dollars and coin,
The exacting template that defines a crest, proclaiming to all whom we cheer for.
The shades of metal for prizes we covet: gold, silver and bronze,
The rainbow to show that we are all human--not just blue and pink.

Colours surround life and death, encompass everything
The colours within ourselves that cannot be described directly;
The glow of a pregnant woman bursting with life.
The pigment of a newborn, fresh from the womb,
The solemn and sallow colours of those dying or freshly departed and
The starkness of bones and teeth left behind.

But there is so much more to discover, those colours we can't see-
White is a colour created of all colours, containing the full spectrum.
Black is the absence of colour, and yet all colours at once,
The UV waves that darken our skin and those too delicate to be viewed.

What more colours could we find?
What names would we give these colours?
What feelings and emotions would they inspire?
What colours would define us all?

A colour can be a symbol of change, defining with it newness and opportunity.
The empty canvas for the artist, fresh paper for the writer-
The shade of fabric so perfect as to become a wardrobe masterpiece
The unshaped metal, as seen by a smith, ready to become something greater.
The garden rows of newly-tilled dirt, awaiting planting and growth.
Each of us, born of colour, both present and absent,
Waiting to be defined, molded, and established-
And yet, totally complete, today as yesterday.

Each day we exist as a colourful masterpiece.
Waiting to be accepted, acknowledged and appreciated-
All colours unique that they will forever envelop us.

Poem Colours
By Michelle T. Lambert

Colours –
Nature has so many colours:
for working and playing,
for living and dreaming,
for singing and dancing.
There's an entire spectrum of colours
that describe sights, moments and feelings...
all expressing life.

Delightful double rainbows of promise,
glorious shapes and colours staging delight,
pastel also bright sunrises and sunsets
streaking across the heavens
on bright mornings, and wondrous nights.

Green's not a primary colour,
yet it exists in so many shades,
like Kelly green, lime, aquamarine,
pea-green vegetables and Jasper's jade-green,
or a beautiful emerald ring,
striking chartreuse flowers seen from afar,
or tasty green olives eaten from a jar.

New leaves and emerging buds
seen in the spring
just makes one want to sing,
soft grass-covered hills for young children
to tickle their toes and, oh well, stain their clothes.

Stately rows upon rows of evergreens,
tall cedars, firs, and spruces blue-green,
slender graceful willows,
unobtrusive Russian olive trees
rustling in the breeze.
Grassy-green moss growing near the sea -
There you'll spot seaweed, quite a delicacy.

Do you like crunchy pistachios?
Notice the insides - now there's a nice green!
Personally I love the colour of fresh mint-green!
And round dark green-speckled melons in the garden
they'll ripen who knows when.

Buttery, finely textured, creamy fleshed fruit,
Its edible casing is green with some pink
We're talking of pears of course,
Tasty to eat, quite anywhere.
Lastly if you're a painter, you'll use Phthalo green:
utilize it to brighten transparent colours
in your daily routine.

Colours of blue, predominantly true,
peacock, indigo, robin's-egg blue:
imagine a beautiful azure sky on a bright summer day,
or deep blue ultramarine that just begs to be seen!
Or sky blue, royal blue, sapphire and teal
Shades of blue and of green; for personal appeal
Add more blue or more yellow, for tints in-between.

Discover blue and purple Morning Glories
a joy to the eye, admire gardens with
lilacs, also orchids in royal colours of
mauve and of plum, not to forget
shades of lavender, violet, and midnight-blue steel.
Observe denim and grape, eggplant, and blue lapis stone
sought after since history for its deep celestial blue tone.

Colours black - like juicy blackberries
and healthy green-black cucumbers,
little girls with jet-black hair wearing
velvet black dresses while eating
black licorice, and pianists playing on black pianos.

Outside children of young years
make loud cheers! They're having fun
wearing Mickey Mouse ears.

Think of quality pewter, an attractive metal -
it's an alloy consisting mostly of tin.
Imagine porpoises with shades of gray on their backs
with white undersides,
ravens and crows out in the yard at the back.

Talk of beautiful slate floors, white gold and silver,
and discarded gray found in the trash.
Charcoal, a light black residue consisting of carbon
and remaining ash, and of course oil,
pitch-black as the night, total absence of light.

Silvery hoar-frost, fresh snow on the ground,
snow-topped huge mountains, a skier's delight,
pristine Easter white lilies, a true sign of spring,
the beauty of pearls, treasured by women and girls.
Think of eggs with cool cream,
priceless ivory parchment, also pure cotton,
porcelain and alabaster, all are sought after.

Red, now there's a warm colour!
Like scarlet and cardinal, dark crimson, too,
folks enjoying a fine claret or
perhaps a glass of Merlot or a sparkling rosé,
often with salmon steaks and lobster-red bakes.
Perhaps there's long-stemmed deep red roses
that add to the occasion 'tween people that are closest.

People delighting in amazing Bing cherries,
luscious thimbled raspberries, gorgeous plump strawberries,
freshly-picked purple plums and succulent apricots -
apples delicious, Macs red and green -
eat one when you wake up, better'n caffeine.
Who can resist watermelon on a hot sunny day,
Adults and children eating away.

Wonder at the regal purple Clematis or the lavender Iris,
so noble, so bold,
the awe of cherry and white apple blossoms,
a thrill in springtime,
such things in life are truly sublime!

Rosy-cheeked children playing near the brick house
with their fire-engine red toys and oh what a noise!

Don't forget gorgeous yellow and pink-tinged roses,
Citrus oranges, lemons and pink grapefruits round,
deep yellow daffodils and sunflowers,
appearing in springtime, then seeds on the ground.
I remember my yellow-tinged canary with white plumes around.
Make peace with dandelions and bees,
they pollinate wildflowers and make honey, if you please.

Sweet juicy peaches, luscious nectarines, too,
carrots and pumpkins with carotene, to name but a few.
All this while gazing at bright burning bushes of
striking red yellow orange maples,
and orange-red berries for birds, on mountain ash trees.
Sunshiny marigolds, rust and saffron,
Terra cotta orange, copper, brass, and gold to don.

Autumn and winter, spring and summertime
show off their brilliance, time after time!

So many colours in nature, a dazzling array -
while thinking of colours, I'm carried away -
pastel, muted, or bright, quite a few
depending, of course, on your point of view.

Can you imagine the world
in shades of just black, white and gray?
I imagine that's all there'd be anyway.
If we didn't have colours, to delight you and me,
would we know life, and all it can be?

Window Walking

Inside Looking Out

By Kathleen Piesse

Window shopping is a term used to describe a familiar activity, done from the outside, looking in; for some, it is a satisfying alternative to actually shopping – i.e. spending money. A less familiar activity, done from the inside, looking out, might be termed window *walking*; for some, it is a satisfying alternative to actual walking – i.e. expending energy.

Consider this: We are at the kitchen sink, inside an east-facing window. Situated at considerable height, our viewpoint overlooks a brief, downward slope which levels out and rises gently for a quarter-mile or so. Then the altitude drops, enough for the lowlands beyond to be hidden from view. A mile or more farther on, the prospect becomes more interesting, since a long, hilly ridge rises upward, like a feature wall. On this wide promontory, sloping fields and scattered groves – here and there marked by little roads curving upward – present intricate patterns, varying in colour and shape, according to the season. Through the imaginative practice of window *walking* one can wander there, amidst nature's pleasant surroundings, expending little more than the energy required to wash the dishes.

Something else for the window *walker* to ponder – of a morning – is the situation of the rising sun progressing through the seasons day by day. In December, around the time of the winter solstice, not only does it rise very late, but so far to the south as to be invisible from this window, unless the walker leans far forward and peers to the right. This is necessary only to satisfy curiosity, however, since one's attention is hijacked by the beauty of its rising light, beaming onto undulating snow through the branches and trunks of a windbreak consisting of stately Northern Poplars. Spread out before us, divided into crazy-quilt patches by the inky shadows of tree trunks and limbs, is a surfeit of abstract pictures in amazing shades of violet and indigo, from almost white through blue-black. So comes another opportunity for the imagination to embark on a fanciful stroll, while we rest for a moment from quotidian tasks.

Though the sunrises, during the two or three weeks before and after the seasonal equinoxes, are beautiful enough in themselves, they lack the painterly skills demonstrated by those of midwinter and midsummer. Still, the window *walker* may take a flight of fancy just before sunup in early spring or fall, provided skies are not too cloudy. Then a surprising number of airplane's jet-trails project, like beacons, across the eastern sky. Illuminated from below the horizon by the invisible sun, each creates its own unique sunrise. Reminded of cities in Saskatchewan and far beyond, as well as the nearer presence of Edmonton, the window *walker* might envision being an airline passenger high in that eastern sky, anticipating a day's work, or an enjoyable visit, upon landing.

Still, from late summer well into autumn – here in Alberta – it is unnecessary for the window *walker* to seek inspiration from sunrises in order to travel via the mind. Then, at any time of day, the colours of nature are breathtaking. At morning and evening they rival the sun's palette and, through the day's middle hours, they accent and provide contrast to clear skies and earthen fields. When rain-wet, they are ethereal. So, regardless of time or weather, any excuse is perfect for looking out the window and partaking of an imaginary autumn walk.

And so the practice of window *walking* provides the opportunity for us to recall the many gifts real walks offer: in winter, the beauty of hoarfrost, and wind-sculpted snowdrifts; in spring the familiar wildflowers – barely large enough to be identified – bravely commencing to grow, then readily recognized in summer by their blossoms and, later, by the fruits of their stalwart efforts to survive and reproduce. We also remember the possibilities offered by Strawberry vine, Raspberry cane, Saskatoon, Chokecherry and Hazelnut bush, and the secretive vine of the Purple Virgin's Bower (Blue Clematis). As summer continues its advance toward autumn, we may delight in recollecting special blossoms once viewed, and delicious fruits once gathered. Visualizing these scenes, we are inspired to repeat, in thought, many pleasant walks over favorite paths.

Window *walking* may also offer gifts to the eye, and to the mind, in the exact moment. We catch sight of a variety of bird species gathering on the young maple immediately outside. Hearing their songs, and observing their flight patterns, we are reminded of names previously learned, and we take pleasure in making them familiar once more. Even Magpies, Crows, Ravens, and Hawks, each with their own distinct way of winging across our sight-line, provide opportunity for us to enjoy a brief, easy return to the practice of birdwatching.

Also in the exact moment, but farther away, deer may be seen browsing for a few hurried moments in the morning dew, then slipping under the fence (yes, under) and out of sight. Much later, gleaming in the waning afternoon sun, a White Tail doe grazes. She seems nonchalant, but all the while she is attending to her fawn, hidden at some distance. A fox, as red as the doe covertly watching it, aims like an arrow for cover in the shelter belt. Nearby, two Eastern Kingbirds, making their annual summer appearance, happily hawk from handy perches on the fence.

Imaginings, memories, actualities – all are available to the window *walker* by the simple act of looking out from the inside.

Metamorphosis
By Alison Whittmire

Once a raindrop
This ripple in the water
Becomes a tidal wave.

H_2O always,
Yet never the same.

Hallelujah – Rain

By Lorelei Roll

The wet – my garden may grow yet.
For too long we have been denied this nourishment.
We have seen forests and cities burn – for rain.
We have yearned – for rain.
Farmers have doubted the sanity
Of planting their crops.
Now they can relax – it is here.
Rain, glorious rain – hallelujah!
Grass and trees can green-up.
Robins can feed on worms.
All the earth's creatures can carry on
In celebration of rain.
Outside my window I hear rain – yes rain!
Yes! I feel the cool breeze on my cheek – I smell
Rain! It soothes my heart – and brain.

Childhood Memories
A Summer Day
By Kathleen Piesse

An ordinary summer afternoon became a special memory the day we hauled the chicken house home to our backward little farm. There had been an auction sale in a neighbouring district and, more out of curiosity than for any need to buy, my two great uncles had attended. When they came puttering home that afternoon, the rest of the family was looking forward to nothing more than one of our aunt's tasty suppers, and a leisurely report of events. So my brother and I were surprised to be hustled into the house, told to wash more than just our hands, change our shirt and blouse – *and* put on socks and shoes. This was exciting; *all* of us were going right back to the sale to collect a purchase!

Before the uncles had finished their first cup of tea – supper would be delayed – my brother and I were ready and waiting in the cluttered farmyard. Surrounded by tumbledown corrals and an odd collection of old fashioned outbuildings and broken-down machinery, we waited near the farm's one concession to modernity: Uncle Roy's big, McCormick Deering tractor. Dwarfed by its high, rubber-tired back wheels, excitedly breathing in the smell of sun warmed grease and fuel, we waited for what seemed forever. Finally, the engine was cranked into roaring life. Then Uncle Dick loaded the two of us and his sister-in-law, Aunt Edna, into his little International truck and we scooted after Uncle Roy and the tractor.

By the time we arrived at our destination, the sale was over but Aunt Edna – delighted at the unexpected pleasure – was still able to visit with a favourite friend. Meanwhile our two uncles, with much help and advice from men at hand, maneuvered the prized purchase onto a pair of strong logs, firmly braced together, providing skids for the building to ride on.

While the tractor was carefully chained to its load, my brother and I examined the interior of the little house. A low, sturdy structure, once painted a pretty green, this one-roomed cabin boasted a lined and insulated interior with a solid wooden floor. The door, of perpendicular tongue-and-groove boards, had a simple thumb latch that could be locked, outside or in, with neat metal turnbuckles. The chimney-hole indicated heating had once been a feature, and there was a ceiling to help keep interior warmth from escaping through the low-pitched, shingled roof. There were a couple of small windows, smeared and grimy. Once, this had been home for someone – perhaps a hired man with a family. There were still a few old children's toys and books, and some outdated newspapers and magazines scattered about.

The sun was setting when our homeward procession finally got underway. Uncle Roy took the lead, proudly gunning the motor of the big tractor as it dragged its burden down the road into the slanting rays. The rest of us followed, again crowded onto the narrow seat of the old truck.

Progress was slow, but the evening was pleasant. With the windows down, we rolled along through pockets of still air, warm from the earlier heat of the day, or through breezes, scented by exhaust fumes and dust. The sounds of our own progress were drowned out by the thrumming roar of the big engine as the tractor laboured before us, dragging the trim little building over the sandy road. Silhouetted by the setting sun, it advanced as smoothly and proudly as a boat moving on a placid river. Dusk was falling when we made the sharp turn onto the steep approach to our gate.

Down into the low land beside the watercourse the tractor plunged, the little building swooping madly after it in a sideways slide. In the truck, all four of us held our breath as, with an abrupt jerk, the building straightened course. Tramping hard on the brake to avoid crashing into the small building, Uncle Dick brought our vehicle to a skidding halt, killing the motor. We could only guess whether his curses were for his own poor driving, or for Uncle Roy's.

Now, tractor and cabin were taking a wild run at the steep hill that marked the beginning of the last tricky stretch of the trail leading to our farmstead. With the truck's motor still off, we watched in fascination for the McCormick Deering to demonstrate its true worth.

Exaggerated by the stillness of the evening and the lay of the land, the tractor's voice sang out. The slower the great machine moved with its burden, the louder the engine roared. Not once did it balk. As it crested the hill it began to move at a brisk clip, and we felt sure Uncle Roy was learning new skills about throttling down and braking, while descending the other side. Our vehicle restarted, we hurried to catch up. What a relief to find all still safely under control when, once again, we had the little shack in sight!

Now the road was no longer steep, but it was narrow and curving as it followed the contours of a boggy area that butted up against the slopes. Worse was a sharp bend around a spring-fed well, its pump nestled beneath dark willows; there the track further narrowed, and was always muddy. This time, we parked deliberately and waited in pregnant silence, praying luck would hold.

The voice of the engine changed continuously as Uncle Roy geared it down again and again, fighting to keep his load moving truly on the slick trail. We held our breath in suspense, worried the huge wheels of the tractor would slip sideways and wipe out the pump, or allow our already beloved little building to become mired.

The big wheels did slip, scars in the mud mute evidence for days afterward. But, as the four of us groaned in despair, providence, or some buried chunk of rock or rotten stump, gave purchase and, first tentatively then triumphantly, forward movement resumed. Now we heard a symphony in dramatic crescendo as Uncle Roy ratcheted the throttle forward, and tractor and little house charged up into the dooryard, to disappear beyond a gentle rise.

Spellbound, we heard the big engine stop abruptly, and backfire twice. A stream of bright orange sparks — blasting from the tractor's exhaust pipe — crested the rise and danced up into the darkened sky. Then, like shooting stars, they disappeared one by one, leaving us in silence.

Legacy

By Jenna Hanger

Hanging from a rusty nail in the rickety horse barn was an old worn-out lasso rope. The cowboy who wielded it had long since passed on, leaving the ranch to his descendants. Back in its glory days expert hands had used the rope nearly every day. It cut through the air landing perfectly around a calf's neck. Pulling tight it would keep the animal secure while the men rushed forward to brand their mark in its hide. The lasso would then get coiled back up where it would wait, like a cobra ready to strike, for its next chance to prove its worth. The shifting nerves of the snorting horse and the strong hands of the cowboy would vibrate through its fiber. Years of progress had rendered this method of work less efficient. Now the lasso sat like an old forgotten friend, a silent witness to the comings and goings in the barn. Its once taut strands were limp, and gifts from the pigeons roosting in the roof decorated the exterior. Dust had settled deep into its threads, turning the colour to a depressed grey. It had become such a part of the barn no one would ever think of moving it. It belonged there much like the windows, the wooden planks and peeling paint. If only that old lasso could speak and educate the people hurrying by about their very own history. It would tell captivating stories of long nights on cattle drives, camping on the trail, fighting through the best of what Mother Nature could conjure… But it just hangs there, a memento of days past.

Relieved

By Robert Swann

Solitary souls with no room to roam
Once I wondered, now I know
The wind gives them voices, they live for the dance
The rain falls in torrents, at Spring's advance
Forest for the trees

Childhood Memories

An Autumn Day

By Kathleen Piesse

For a child, nothing is more delightful than awakening on a morning in late autumn to find the outdoors blanketed in fresh snow ... unless it is to be in the midst of the event as it happens. I particularly remember one fall evening when, as my great uncle listened to his old battery-powered radio, a weather forecast predicting cold temperatures and a heavy snowfall promised exactly that opportunity.

The weather was exceptionally good all summer and fall, and an early, abundant harvest had just been completed. As a result of such superb fortune, it was necessary to postpone taking up the later-maturing produce from our large vegetable garden. Now, if the weatherman was accurate, we were faced with having to race an Alberta storm for possession of this bounty. Before bedtime, plans were made to start work in the garden promptly after an early dinner the next day. In our household of five, at least two members – my brother and I – fell asleep happily anticipating such prospects.

The next morning dawned crystal-bright, and beautiful as only an autumn morning in Alberta can be. Everyone hurried to complete regular chores in record time. Then the faithful team of workhorses, their well-deserved rest after the harvest cut short, was brought in from pasture, and my brother and I were sent scurrying in search of forks, spades and other essential tools, as noisy to-dos about 'where is this?', and 'have you seen that?' arose. Soon every empty tub and bucket, every old box and sack on the place, was loaded into the wagon box.

Precisely at noon, our assault on the garden commenced, the entire household projecting itself into a frenzy of potato ploughing, carrot digging, turnip pulling and cabbage lopping.

We children were not slaves to the work on our backward old farm. Considered more of a nuisance than a help where choring was concerned, my brother was usually left happily playing imaginary games in and around the house. And, though preferring to be outdoors amidst the activities of the farmyard or wandering the fields and woods, I was encouraged toward girlish pastimes, like piano lessons, reading and fancy-work. That day, however, both of us were expected to work alongside the three adults who comprised the rest of our odd little family.

Each of our two great uncles had his own farm on adjacent land, so it was possible for them to help one another with certain operations. However, they were an opinionated pair, and this happened less often than might be expected. Fortunately, the elder had a wife to help him and the younger, somewhat more progressive than his brother – and scornful of the latter's backward ways – considered himself capable of managing alone, though some would beg to differ. Although he had his own small, well-constructed, reasonably modern house – better than the one in which the rest of us lived – he seldom stayed there. Instead, he was given a room, a reserved place at table, and treatment as their equal, in the home of the married couple. So, on occasions such as this, when the family's food supply was in jeopardy, he had little choice but to pitch in and do his part. This was small payment in return for laundry done and shirts ironed, and for being served only foods that agreed with his touchy stomach, whilst using his own particular preference in china and cutlery. No wonder his elder brother called him "The Prodigal Son."

On that, or any other day, our great aunt was the hardest worker of the three middle-aged people with whom we two youngsters lived. Even now I see her under the hot afternoon sun, face streaming sweat beneath the brim of a man's battered Fedora, housedress and inevitable bib-apron clinging to her damp form as she put her all into the tasks at hand. Hurrying about, skirts flying, strong bare knees showing over cotton hose knotted above her calves, she directed my brother and me. We were inspired by her good example, and by her presence.

The three of us pulled armfuls of dry potato tops and lugged them to the edge of the garden to clear the way for the elder uncle to bring on the team and the walking-plow to turn over the potato row. Not all of the potatoes were laid bare, so the younger uncle came along with a fork, bringing up from the dark pungent earth the deeper growing tubers. All were left to dry in the sunshine and the freshening southeast breeze – a breeze signaling a change in the weather, and urging us on to greater effort.

By the time the carrots and turnips were topped and the cabbages trimmed, the potatoes were dry, ready to be loaded and hauled to the house for storage in the cellar. Now, the horses were put to work pulling the wagon, which we called "The Democrat", though others might term it "The Bennett Buggy". Named for the politics of a previous time which made it necessary for farmers to give up their motorized vehicles, this conveyance consisted of a shallow box installed on the running gear of an old car. It was converted to true horsepower by the installation of a wagon pole. Given the relatively small wheels, the box was low-slung, making loading easier and transport safer than using the high-wheeled grain wagon.

Having plenty of food stored for winter was essential for our family. Too much, in fact, better describes the amounts of canned fruit, vegetables, and even meat that crowded onto the shelves in our dark, dusty cellar. In addition, piles of potatoes, boxes of carrots packed in sand, and heaps of turnips and cabbages crammed the space beneath the kitchen floor each fall. Many trips down the garden hill with the overloaded wagon were necessary this autumn afternoon. As each slow, winding journey was completed, the sense of urgency increased, for clouds darkened the sky, and the temperature was dropping.

Chosen by the elder great uncle in some sort of wise/eccentric fit – when he was intent upon protecting his food source from the ravages of Alberta's late spring and early fall frosts – the location of this cornucopia of cultivation was most inconvenient. High on a side hill at considerable distance from the house, a footpath led directly to the spot, upward from the spring, through a thick growth of aspens. But the only way to get there from the house, by team and wagon, was along the sloping flank of this formidable Parkland knob. Doubtless, there was much cause for consternation in the minds of the three adults struggling to beat the approaching storm.

Of course, my brother and I were forbidden to ride atop the loads of produce as they were hauled to the house; that would have been much too dangerous. But it was exciting for us to imagine the loaded wagon tipping over, sending vegetables rolling down the side hill, scattering them through patches of fine prairie wool and thick buck brush. We held our breath and bit our knuckles, watching from a well-chosen viewpoint as the steadfast teamster – the elder great uncle – with coaxing, soothing words and a firm hold on the lines, eased the big horses downward, keeping them to a back-slanting walk. Still, they barely managed to brake the heavily-loaded wagon as it threatened to push them into a dangerous trot. With each trip, we breathed a little easier when they were turned onto the trail leading safely down past the spring and into the yard beyond.

The snow came before the last load was completely rescued. Great, quarter-sized flakes dappled the horses' round haunches and clung to their thick manes. Weighty blobs plopped onto the binder canvasses momentarily covering the last piles of produce where they lay on the tumbled earth. Delighted, my brother and I spun about in the kaleidoscope of whiteness, our world blurred by dizziness and the moving curtain of snow. It mattered little that we were improperly clothed for the elements. We were hot with bliss, and hardly felt the soaking cold. I remember my surprise when, upon my great aunt's admonishment, I looked down at my feet to see them sockless and red, shod only in the sandals I had donned that morning.

Shooed to the house to put on warmer clothing, we soon returned to the garden to gather the hand-tools before they were snowed under and lost. Emerging from the trees atop the garden hill, we climbed between strands of the barb-wire fence just in time to see the last load leaving the garden gate. Even as we located the scattered forks and hoes, snow covered the lumpy soil and the refuse strewn all about. Heads missing, the remains of cabbages were unrecognizable, while other discarded vegetation and clods of earth joined them in an undulating, broad sculpture in white.

Tired and happy, we carried our awkward burdens down through the silent woods to the old house. As we emerged from the trees near the spring, we saw smoke from the kitchen range drifting upward from the battered, tin stovepipe. It mingled with, then disappeared into the swirling snowflakes. Below, the younger great uncle stuffed the last of the garden's bounty through the cellar door while, over at the barn, the elder cared for the exhausted horses.

Ravenous, we couldn't help thinking of the supper being prepared by our great aunt. We visualized the luscious stew, bright with chunks of fresh vegetables, redolent with spices and onion, and fortified with an entire two-quart sealer of succulent canned beef. There would be thick slices of homemade bread topped by a layer of salty butter, and we would have fruit preserves for dessert.

The five of us – this odd little family – were about to celebrate the completion of a very important undertaking. But, for me, the real celebration was about having been out, on that special day, in the very midst of the season's most thrilling, first snowfall.

The Buck

By Jenna Hanger

It was cold. Not minus thirty cold, but cold enough to require a toque, mitts and several layers of clothing. I had removed my mitts so I could wrap my hands properly around the gun. I liked the feel of it, heavy and cool against me, securely jammed against my shoulder. The safety was on, but the magazine was locked with three bullets ready and waiting. I had more in the breast pocket of my jacket but I wouldn't be fast enough to reload if I needed them right away. Inexperience made me clumsy, as well as handling the right handed-gun when I was left-handed. The curse of being the only southpaw in a large right-handed family meant that very few things were actually made for me. I shifted my position slightly, never looking away from the bush ahead. I was leaning against a fence post with my knees propped up to better stabilize the rifle. The frost bitten ground was turning me numb as it seeped through my layers.

We started this morning when it was still dark, driving around to the most popular places where there was usually frequent wildlife activity: me, Dad and one of my older sisters. I enjoyed that part, cruising around, straining to pick out movement from the sea of brown and spidery bare trees sitting in clusters throughout the fields. Dad was a pro, he could pick out the slightest movements and identify what sort of animal it was. My eyes constantly played tricks on me, so I never trusted what I saw. Dad would suddenly hit the brakes and grab the binoculars, "Look right there! See them?" I wouldn't but immediately we would open the doors and hop out, trying to train our scopes on the targets.

"Does," he said, before I could pick them out. With those words the excitement would fade a little. We never shot does.

"See them, Jen? Get your scope on them." It was good practice to find the deer in your scope, important when trying to train your reaction time of getting them in the crosshairs. I closed one eye and moved my head back and focused, trying to eliminate the blackness around my vision to see what he was seeing. Then, there! Invisible at first, perfectly blending into her surroundings a deer stood frozen in my sights, looking right at me. For a breathless moment we are locked together, then she turns and leaps away, disappearing from sight.

They are the only ones we have seen so far this morning.

I am today's focus. It would be my first kill, having turned fourteen this year I was finally the legal age to hunt. So Dad dropped me off on top of a small hill overlooking a valley with clumps of trees. He drove the truck down with my sister, where they parked and got out, slung their guns over their shoulders and walked around the other side of dense bush to crash through and hopefully scare out anything living towards me.

I have permission to shoot anything with horns. I have both a whitetail and mule deer tag with my name on it. Dad also left me with careful instructions to never shoot unless I have a clear target, never shoot over a hill and never shoot if I don't know where everyone is.

I tighten my grip and exhale, a small puff of breath rising before me. The sky above is just starting to turn a pale shade of pink as the sun is slowly greeting the frozen land. Birds sing back and forth as an icy breeze plays across my face, paying particular attention to my nose and finger tips which I can barely feel.

There! My heart jolts against my throat as two deer explode from the bushes. Doe, doe... I take the safety off and press the gun hard against my shoulder. Another doe joins them, and then...he comes. Tossing his head, antlers gleaming in the morning light.

I have my scope on him, following his movement with my finger on the trigger. Pull it, shoot! But the enormity of the act stops me cold. I hold in my hand a weapon, and in this moment I have the power to end a life. It's an incredible, intimidating feeling. Buck Fever is what the hunters call it, when you're so full of adrenaline you can't actually pull the trigger.

The buck pauses for a moment, staring vainly around. It's my last chance. Aim above the shoulder, below the neck. I hold my breath and squeeze.

25

The shot rings out, echoing across the valley. The impact jars my entire body. My ears are ringing and my shoulder immediately starts to throb. I saw him jump. I hit him. He is running, but I hit him.

I stand up exhilarated, not sure what to do next. I see Dad emerge from the bushes and sprint to the truck. He roars over and picks me up, barely waiting for me to shut the door before we take off in pursuit. My sister, I assume, is still in the bush.

We spot the buck right ahead of us heading towards another treeline. Dad slows as the deer tires and limps into the covering. Following Dad's instructions we get out and creep towards the trees, quiet as we can, following the dark trail of blood. I see him ahead of me, lying down with his head up. His antlers aren't huge. Dad says it's a three point whitetail. But I don't care. I lift my rifle again. We are so close I don't even need the scope. Bracing myself for the impact, I hesitate only a moment and pull the trigger for a second time. I was ready for the jolt, but the sound still takes me by surprise. I hit him clean, and he falls completely down. Gone.

I did it. I am shaking. We draw closer and I see my prize. He is beautiful, still warm from the life that was in him.

"Good job!" Dad exclaimed, clapping my shoulder. "That was a good shot!"

"Thanks," I breathe, kneeling down beside him. My emotions feel like they are fighting against each other. The thrill of the accomplishment beat against my chest, but a sad, dull ache is also there for this creature which minutes ago had been strong and mighty, leaping across the plains with grace, leading his herd around the prairies. It is a powerful thing, what we humans can do.

Thirteen Ways of Looking at a Pine Tree

By Judy Jackson

1
A bold pine tree in winter
Moves graciously in summer
2
The grey squirrel
Steals another cone
Slinks down the trunk
Feeling sly and smug
The pine tree
Let's him feel that way
3
Pines line like
Soldiers in a row
Arresting the winter snow
4
A green canopy
Swung over a white rabbit
5
A crusted sailor
The Torrey pine
Roots itself in
California sand
Its bark brittle and unsteady
Blasted by storm
Burned by sun
6
A wood-giver
A fire-builder
A shade-giver
A Sunday paper
7
From the corner
Of a Christmas morning
The jack pine leans
Puffed out in its finery
Offering its presence to the world

8
The sugar pine clings
To its dry mountain slope
A sweet photograph
9
A Tom Thomson pine
10
Campfire casts an eerie light
On primordial majesty
11
Have you ever inhaled the scent?
Of a pine tree
After a spring rain?
12
Ancient poetry is tucked among the pine boughs
Cathedral aisles
And bearded images
Enchanted rhyme
As precious as the pine itself
13
Perched on charred ponderosa
A woodpecker surveys the gutted woodland
While grey skeletons reach for blue sky

Morning Walk
Mind Pictures
By Kathleen Piesse

I am fond of being out in Nature, and I recognize my need to walk in every season. Always there are interesting things to observe and to understand; beautiful pictures that I wish my paint brush could duplicate on paper, or my camera capture in photographs. And, time and time again, I must acknowledge that the mind, a tool thousands of times better equipped to create images, within itself, than can ever be duplicated on paper or canvas, is the device by which I am seeing. I am thankful that, occasionally, I enjoy the gift of seeing in such a way.

So it was, recently, on my Shelter-belt Trail. As I tramped around and around, placing my feet in my own rough tracks, Nature's gift began its process. Then I saw the ethereal colours of the shadows accenting my footprints in the white-on-white drifts, and the prettier, bluer shadows cast on smooth snow by dead grass, branches and tree-trunks. Fainter shadows, on the pristine canvas, revealed the gentle undulations of Nature's fleecy blanket, covering and comforting the sleeping plants and the frozen earth beneath.

Under that comforting mantle there was, I knew, life. Witness the occasional tiny footprints of four-legged creatures – Least weasels or field mice, perhaps – burrowing either upward, or down, leaving their distinctive trails. And there was also death. Witness the imprint of a bird's wing and tail feathers and the empty, dark hole in the deep drift, indicating a predator had found prey.

Just as interesting was evidence that, from the hay meadow, a Coyote had entered the path about half-way down the north side. Its tracks followed my own spoor, towards the barnyard, and then back in the other direction – not prepared to enter occupied territory? – all the way to the far end of the shelter belt. There, the trunk of an almost-fallen Northern Poplar grows against the ground for a few feet, forming a place for me to sit, before it turns and heads true and straight, toward the sky. The wild dog evidently examined this bench with care, though I saw no evidence of its presence being marked. I suppose it is too early for the mating season, and the irresistible urge such a creature would then have, to indicate its territorial instincts in an obvious way.

The delicate imprints made by those wild, canine feet were perfectly formed, though the weight of the animal must have been hardly enough to press its toes into my own packed trail. But there they were, to be truly seen, noted and imprinted in my mind. And I still have this and the other pictures from my morning walk to look at, any time I wish to remember them. How long can I keep them there, I wonder?

Such lovely mind-pictures are fleeting. But I shall keep them, even after they are gone...as long as I am able, again, to walk my snowy Shelter-belt Trail.

Who Gave Me that Valentine?

By Judy Moody

Miss Arnesson's voice drives everyone to distraction. I'd rather listen to fingernails scratchin' on the blackboard than her voice trying to talk over all of us.

"Now claaass," she screeched as we got ready to scram when the three o'clock bell rang. "It's Valentine's Day tomorrow so don't forget your cards and treats to share."

"What are you bringin', Evalina?" Misty asked me while struggling into her stiff raincoat.

"My mom is making brownies with red icing hearts on top."

"Oh, man! I love your mom's brownies; they're so fudgy," Bubblubble chimed in. "Make sure I get some of them, will ya?" And off he ran to catch up with the other boys.

"Okay," I called after him. "What are you bringin', Misty?"

"Don't tell anyone," she whispered, "but my mom has figgered out how to make RED popcorn balls and shape them into hearts. She saw the recipe in that ladies' magazine she gets every month in the mail."

"They sound amazing! I promise not to tell."

"Who are you giving valentine cards to?" Misty asked.

"I never tell. Never. I always sign the ones to girls but never the ones I give to boys. I don't want to be teased forever – 'Ooooo, you're in love with h, uh, him. When you gonna marry him?' Nope, can't tell even you."

"Okay, okay, don't blow your top!" she said. "Which boy or boys do you want to get a card from?"

"If I tell you that, you'll know who I'm giving cards to, won't you?" I yelled.

"Fine! I'm not tellin' you neither then," said Misty, pouting.

The next day, Valentine's Day, everyone showed up wearin' red and bringin' a box or bag of goodies. We couldn't wait 'til after lunch, but we had to.

"Trials before treats," teacher said and busted our heads with arithmetic and spelling quizzes all morning long. We did get to pin up the red hearts on lace paper doilies that we had made yesterday and left out for the glue to dry.

"Now eat your lunch food first," Miss Arnesson squawked as the lunch bell rang and we scrambled to stare at all the treats she had lined up on the craft table under the windows. There were little white cupcakes with a cinnamon heart on top, little plastic baskets filled with cinnamon hearts, of course red popcorn balls and my mom's brownies (which were grabbed up first). Also marshmallows covered in red sprinkles, pink heart-shaped cookies and chocolate hearts wrapped in gold foil - those were from the teacher herself. Boy, you never saw boloney sandwiches and cheese sandwiches gobbled down so fast in all your life!

"You-all drink your milk too," said Miss A. "You want strong teeth and bones, don't you?"

"Who cares," mumbled Stilts, "just let us get to the good stuff, will ya?"

"Just let us get to the Valentines cards," whispered Misty. "Someone here is waiting for a special one, isn't she?"

I poked her.

Once we had pigged-out on treats and washed our hands, (Miss Screechy insisted), we slit open the red crepe paper-covered box full of Valentine cards. We girls were all excited. The boys were bored, wishing they could have more treats. I swear Bubblubble would have licked the plates if he'd been allowed. That boy is always hungry!

Four students were chosen to play Cupids and deliver all the cards. Miss Arnesson had made little ponchos for them to wear with red bows and arrows painted on them. Of course, only girls volunteered to do this.

It was fun to turn the cards over and see if, or who, had signed them. Many of the cards were the same because there's not much selection in a small town like ours. Only the drug store and grocery store sell them and they both get the same two books of cut-out cards.

Anyway, the boys usually got the plainer, un-mushy ones and we girls got the frillier ones – from other girls mostly, but I did get one that wasn't signed except for a squiggly X. I quickly looked around the room to see if one of the boys was lookin' at me. Nope. Some of them were turning red in the face and groaning if they got one signed by a girl. I peeked out of the corner of my eye to see if my special "arrow" had reached its mark. He never made a sign that it had.

But who gave me the one that had a smiling bee and said, "You're a Honey, Bee mine Valentine" and that squiggly X? Who,who,who?

I thought about it all afternoon. I kept sneakin' looks at each and every boy in the room but carefully so that teacher and nosy old Misty didn't notice, but no boy was lookin' at me in an interested way. So, he's playing hard-to-find-out is he? Well, I guess I'll have to go into detective mode, won't I, I said to myself.

Right after school, I walked up behind my first suspect – Ringaling. I always thought he kind of liked me.

"I know it was you," I whispered right behind his head.

Ringaling jumped half a foot, spun around and said "Listen, don't tell on me! Don't tell and I'll give you this brand new pencil, okay? Here!" and he ran away fast before I could even find out what it was he DID do! But I got a new pencil anyway, even if it wasn't him who gave me the mystery Valentine card.

Who could it be then? So, I saw Stilts bouncing his baseball off the school wall and I wandered by him but not stopping or looking right at him. "It was you, wasn't it?" I said out of the side of my mouth, between the ball hittin' the wall and smackin' into his baseball mitt.

"What?" he squawked. "You couldn't have seen me, it was miles from here! Please, don't tell my mom or I'll be in big trouble! Look, here's a quarter that I found. You can have it if you promise not to tell!" And he flipped me the quarter and took off for home like he had a tiger on his tail!

Well, I still didn't know who my secret admirer was, but I was happy to have a new pencil AND a quarter to spend all on myself. I passed Lanky Toes in the hall the next day. "I know what you did and I'm going to tell everyone," I said very softly, looking into his eyes. Lanky Toes just fainted dead away onto the hall floor he was so scared. I quickly helped him up and took him to the nurse's office. Just before we got there he said in a low, sad voice "Don't tell, Evalina. I didn't mean to, it was a big mistake and I already put it back. Don't tell or my Pa will wallop me good. Here, take my lunch dessert. It's a Hershey bar, they're real good. Please don't tell, please."

Well it obviously wasn't him either but that Hershey bar WAS delicious. Seems like the blackmail business was doin' just fine, but I was beginnin' to feel guilty myself. After all, those boys couldn't have done anything worse than snitchin' corn out of a field or lettin' the air outa some mean guy's tires or tellin' a fib to blame someone for somethin' they did and gettin' away with it. Anyways, after tryin' "I saw what you did with my own eyes" on Snerk and gettin' nothin' but a blank stare, I just plain gave up.

The very next day, I was waitin' my turn after Blue Eyes at the water fountain when he turned his head and said, all the while pretendin' to still be drinkin' water, "Well, will you bee my honey?"

I about dropped dead right then and there! The cutest boy in my room sent me that wonderful Valentines card. How did I not see it on his face? Then I suddenly realized why. He sits right behind me and my neck just doesn't swivel around that far!

He stepped aside then and as I bent down to drink I whispered, "Yes, I will but it's gotta be a secret or we'll get teased to death, okay?"

"Okay," he said. "We're too young to get married anyway."

Snow Eater
By Judy Jackson

Wind cuts through
the arched portal of western sky
on the move
from another place
a warmer place

A small force at first
skims
the crusted snow banks
that lie
'neath the winter sun
swells

across dormant wheat fields
weaves
through poplar trees
snags the odd leaf dried and
dangling
discards it quickly

hurries
over fieldstone
never stops
to consider the landscape
moves
up hill   down valley
wipes out
any recent taste of winter

Reaches the yard
wraps
'round the verandah
squeezes
between floorboards
up the faded shiplap
temperature rises
minus 10 to plus 15 in less than 20 minutes

Banks of snow
recede
leaving dirty drool
a weathered trellis
drips liquid
from diamond contours

a figure steps out
to inspect the afternoon
her face
 tilted
lifts her arms
crosses
them overhead
A shield
she closes her eyes
feels the smug gust
rush through her
the warmth defies the January day

More than a breeze now
the wind
pushes
forces her arms
'round the verandah post
a heady scent
of earth and wet
infuse the air

"I am the Snow Eater!"
the wind
wails
releasing a secret
too large to handle

The Silver Lining
By Robert Swann

Sun breaks through
      Blue sky is enlightened
Last week I saw a robin
      Then there were five
Spring has sprung
      So much has changed
Today the sun smiles
      From the ice-free lake
Forgotten details
      Keep me looking up
My song is new
      Not of sorrow
Note and tune
      Happiness and joy
Easier
Travels and responsibilities
I'm Thankful

Potato Chip Seagull

By Lori M. Feldberg

The seagull flitted to and fro
Dark in the night, black as a crow
Across the intersection bright
Bird eyes glint back in my headlights.

Silly bird, scavenging at night
Not well endowed with good night sight
He frequently turned his back on me
The seagull then was hard to see.

Dairy Queen draws birds with a knack
The seagull sprints forwards and back
Tasty chips spilled there perhaps
Thus he runs intersection laps.

I could just see him duck to pluck
From the pavement fare DQ chuck
The traffic light, it turned to green
Ready to go forth, I was keen.

Undeterred he kept frantic pace
Those darn greasy chips he gives chase
Enticing him to flaunt the danger
Vehicle mayhem no stranger.

He dips and bobs, tail up and down
With bird-like motion, acts the clown
His head rears higher, he's just so wee
Drawing close I could finally see.

Naught but a potato chip bag
Imposter in the wind, can't lag
I laugh and continue to mull
O're my potato chip seagull.

WOW

By Robert Swann

High above the lonely island
The golden one returns each summer
Sharpening of skill with a shocking splash
Splendour of surprise catches him
Flying away with his catch

Cry Foul

By Patricia Mary O'Neill

My mother killed birds. She wouldn't hurt a fly, yet she killed birds. It was never really her fault, to be sure, but somehow if there was a bird around, its life was in mortal danger.

My first memory of such an incident was the summer of 1959 when I turned seven years old. My parents had given me a yellow parakeet for my birthday. I named him Malcolm. What a beautiful thing he was. I don't know if I slept much those first few days, I just couldn't stop looking at him.

On the third day, somewhere around 3 a.m., Malcolm got out of his cage. That was my fault. I wanted so much to stroke those sunlight-yellow feathers.

When I opened the door, Malcolm scurried to the back of the cage. I tried to reassure him with my hushed words, "It's okay, little fella, I won't hurt you."

I reached inside. When my hand was all the way in, he freaked out. Knowing there was no escape, he did the only thing a bird can do; he bit down hard on my index finger. I yelped and yanked my hand out. He came out with it, still attached - the bird and my finger, thankfully.

Malcolm flew up, feathers askance, then he was out the bedroom door.

I tried to capture him and almost did, just outside my parents' bedroom, but as I closed my fingers around his little body, the only thing I grasped was a tail feather. He escaped between the railings and fluttered down.

I couldn't wake my parents to tell them what happened because I had promised them I would not do the thing I did.

I slunk back to my room, took my Ray-O-Vac flashlight in hand and crept down over the stairs, making sure to straddle the edges so the steps wouldn't creak. My finger stung.

I searched everywhere but after what seemed like forever, I gave up, went back to my bed, exhausted with worry; I fell fast asleep.

The next morning, I awoke to my mother's screams and ran downstairs to see what all the commotion was about. Then I remembered Malcolm.

I saw feathers on the floor and the look of horror on my mother's face. Frantically, she tried to turn off the vacuum cleaner but it kept whirring.

She looked at me, at the feathers, then at the end of the vacuum hose. My mother yelled out for my father.

"Bill, Bill, come quick."

A few seconds later, my father appeared - his face half shaven, a look of alarm in his eyes.

"What is it, what's the matter, Clare?" he asked glancing from her to me.

"I've sucked up Malcolm! I was cleaning behind the curtains and the next thing I know there's a squawk, Malcolm's on the end of the hose and just like that he disappeared inside. I can't shut it off and now..." she stopped speaking and looked over at me, mortified.

My father hauled the plug out of the wall, broke open the canister of our Singer Roll-a-Magic vacuum cleaner to retrieve Malcolm from amongst the dust bunnies.

"Damn!" was the only word he muttered. My mother started to cry. I just stood there, weighted to the carpet, my mouth agape.

"Go to your room, now!" he ordered and I turned and ran up the stairs, but not before I heard him say, "Honey, I think the bird's caught in the hose."

I wasn't allowed to view the remains.

My mother felt so guilty about Malcolm that she never questioned or reprimanded me. Later that night, my father caught me going through the garbage. I had just opened the paper bag that contained Malcolm's broken body when he called out for me to stop.

I was always a curious child.

I moped around for days, sulking, until my parents came home with another yellow bird. Except for my finger, I hadn't really felt that attached to Malcolm, so I was consoled when his look-alike arrived.

I had Gypsy for a few years until *he* mysteriously disappeared. My mother told me that he somehow got out of his cage and flew out the window. She explained that perhaps Gypsy would be happier if he were free to live out his life amongst other birds.

The next day my father brought home a turtle. There were no more birds after that.

When I was a ten, my family took a road trip to Alaska. My father had driven for twelve hours straight, though we did have a few pit stops along the way. My mother, concerned my father would fall asleep at the wheel, convinced him to let her take over.

Reluctantly he agreed and fell asleep shortly thereafter. In the back seat, I put a pillow between myself and the window then pulled a crocheted orange and brown afghan over me and soon nodded off.

I awoke to an enormous jolt (that flung me onto the floor) and my mother's screams. She slammed on the brakes.

"Damn, Bill. It's a bird, a damn bird!" My mother, who never swears was frantic and angry. She beat her hands against the steering wheel. "Can you believe it? I've killed another bloody bird!"

"Mom, Mom, what happened? Are we okay?" It was pitch-black so I had no idea what was going on.

Dad, finally alert, asked her what had happened.

Muttering under her breath, she threw open the driver's side door, got out and proceeded to the back of the vehicle. "See for yourself," she called back.

Father and I exited the car and walked around to the back. There were two white feathers stuck in the metal strapping above the right rear passenger side window. On the ground, ten feet behind the car, a big white bird was flopping around, making an awful sound. Clearly it wasn't dead.

We looked at it, then at Mom.

"What do you mean you killed another bird?" I asked.

"What?" my mother said.

"You said you killed *another* bird."

My mother looked suddenly sheepish and uncomfortable.

"Seriously Frankie, you're not going to grill me right here and now are you? I'm pretty upset and I don't know what I'm saying."

My father interrupted. "We've got to get this creature in the car and see if we can find someone to help it."

"You're not serious?" my mother said, indignant.

"It's okay," my father replied. "Frankie and I'll figure it out. Frankie, give me your blanket. We'll wrap it good and tight around him. Once he's bound up, he should calm down. Now come on and help me."

I did as my father asked and an hour later, in Juneau, Alaska we stopped at the police station and they directed us to a nearby veterinarian who assured us that the bird, a snowy owl, was only stunned and would be perfectly okay. There was a good chance he'd be released back into the wild the very next day.

We were all relieved, especially Mom.

It took some convincing on my father's part to talk my mother out of turning the car south and heading home. We had a good breakfast and hit the road again, my father behind the wheel the rest of the way.

We made it home, safe and sound two weeks later, with a carload of stories to tell about our Alaskan adventure. No one mentioned the owl.

When I was about to turn twelve I asked if I could have another bird for my birthday.

"Under no circumstances," my usually accommodating mother declared. From the tone of her voice, I knew better than to argue. I figured my mother mustn't like birds after all.

The morning of my birthday I awoke to a scruffy bundle of fur barking from the foot of my bed. My parents had seen an advertisement in the local newspaper for miniature Collies and had bought one the day before.

I had my very own little Lassie that I called Yogi after my favorite pitcher Yogi Berra. In the seven years that expired before I headed off to college, Yogi never had a single mishap.

When I returned home for visits, it was clear who ran the household. My mother was at Yogi's beck and call. She spoiled him terribly. My father attested to that fact as he had been relegated to the edge of the bed, just so Yogi didn't feel hemmed in.

"This darn dog runs the roost," he declared. "I spend more time in the dog house than he does," my father laughed as he cuddled with Yogi on the lazy boy.

A car pulled up outside. Yogi's ears shot straight up.

"Who's that?" my father asked in a high pitched voice.

Yogi struggled to break from his grip, yelped frantically and looked expectantly at the front door. Mom walked in, Yogi barked, his little body quivered with excitement and his tail wagged furiously.

"Look what I got for my good little boy," she said in a tone usually reserved for babies.

From a bag she pulled out a yellow plush toy - a bird, almost the size of Yogi. He growled and sunk his teeth into its neck.

"That's my boy," my mother declared. "Have at it."

She looked up, saw me standing there and blushed.

"Oops! Hi honey," she said, straightened up and patted down her dress. "I didn't see you there."

I raised my eyebrows and smiled. "Obviously!"

She walked over and hugged me.

Later that afternoon I helped my father dig up an area of the yard just inside the back fence for a raised bed where they could plant herbs and vegetables. My mother supervised the dig.

When my shovel brought up a wad of fabric, I flicked it off to the side. It unraveled and out fell the skeletal remains of a bird.

"Oh no!" my mother exclaimed. It was then I learned what had really happened.

Gypsy had met with fowl play when he accidentally drowned in a load of wash. Clever bird that he was, he managed to free himself from his cage and find his way into the laundry basket. It wasn't until my mother put the clothes through the ringer that she discovered the soggy bulge.

She was mortified once again that she was the cause of yet another bird's demise. She didn't bother to unwind my father's boxers to see for sure that it was Gypsy; there was no mistaking the beak that protruded from the elastic at the top of the waist band.

She wrapped the bird and boxers in the sports section of that day's unread newspaper and, when he came home, had my father bury it in the back yard.

All those years later, clearly traumatized *yet again*, she burst into tears and ran into the house. I shoveled up the decomposed corpse and reinterred it and filled in the hole.

After supper my mother said she didn't have the heart to tell me what really happened. She felt so guilty. It seemed kinder to let me believe that Gypsy went to be with his own kind.

She wasn't the only one feeling guilty. Shortly after we got Yogi, he and I were playing in the back yard. He ran behind the rose bush and was there for a long time. When I finally went to see what he was up to, that's when I saw the remains for the first time.

I had taught Gypsy how to open his cage and it was my fault he had escaped. Although I never knew how he got from my room to the back yard, I realized my parents had tried to protect me from the truth.

Now it was my turn to come clean. The relief on my mother's face was evident.

The next spring my father and I finally finished that raised garden, but this time in a different part of the yard.

The Miracle: A Sonnet

By Michelle T. Lambert

When I first saw them, oh they were so dear -
Had seemed so long since I had felt such glee
They caused grown men to tremble at the knee
And made all smile and often shed a tear.
Their coming brought such cheer to us those years.
They seemed so precious, wouldn't you agree,
This wondrous joy that finally came to me.
How they would change my life it was unclear.

All the pain was not in vain, bittersweet -
They were my sons, my only Valentines
Tiny, so fragile and smelling so sweet
For them I felt awe, a sense of divine
In overflowing happiness complete
A miracle: these new born babes of mine.

The Year We Was Heroes

By Judy Moody

It was too hot to spit. Me and my whole gang was splayed out under the willow tree down by the crick, like bowling pins after a strike was just throwed. We was just too dang hot and wilted to even pull off our clothes and jump in. It was so hot, I swear I heard the grass hiss from the metal clip on the back of my suspenders when I laid down.

I still had to laugh though when Lanky Toes plunked down and those big long toes of his were pointing up to the sky. Then Blue Eyes, Snerk, Nest Head, Ringaling, and Bubblubble started in laughin' too and even Lanky Toes caught the fit. By the time we quit we were hotter than ever, but never mind. It felt good. It always feels good to laugh 'til you're fit to bust.

Then Snerk (that's the noise he makes when he sniffs up his boogers) asked "What were we laughing about?" and we started in laughing again. Not so long this time – we was too dang tired and our jaws and our sides were hurting from it all. Seems like there actually is such a thing as too much of a good thing. I mean like one too many pieces of Aunt Grete's dark chocolate fudge. You just get sugared out. Know what I mean? Your mouth wants to turn inside out and get hosed off.

There we were, a sorry lookin' bunch of ten year olds, of no particular use to anyone. We was out of school and with no real design for our school break except to enjoy sweet, hot, empty days and cool, lush, frog and lightnin'- bug-hunting evenings. So that's what we were doin'. That and nothin' more. Life was sweet.

Just as I was deciding whether to go to sleep or git up the gumption to undress and swim, I heard somethin'. Well, actually, what caught my ear was hearing nothing first. The birds shut up, sudden-like. There was a skittering in the grass – snakes and such skedaddlin'. Then I heard the voices – men's voices – mean-soundin' voices, comin' from that little hollow down by the roots of this here willow.

I raised my head and looked over at my pals. Nest Head was lookin' right into my eyes. He put his finger on his lips. Seemed like the rest of the guys were asleep so it was up to Nest Head and me to investigate. We rolled over onto our bellies and hauled ourselves through the grass, like them commandoes we'd seen in the movies, over to the edge of the bank o' the crick. That's when we saw them; bad guys, bank robbers, maybe murderers even!

Ugly as sin they was, in dark, dirty clothes and beat-up hats. Three of 'em was sittin' on the ground. The tall, skinny one was standin' up and wavin' a gun! Wow, the hair on the back of my neck was standin' straight up and Nest Head's eyes was as big as saucers, seemed like. I'd never seen a handgun in actual use before; mostly just Pa's rifle and shotgun which he uses for meat huntin' and skeerin' off pesky critters what's after our chickens. This was serious stuff. And Mr. Tall and Skinny was holdin' a bag – a bag with the name of our bank on it.

We wriggled our way backwards to the willow, which is twice as hard as doin' it frontwards, take my word for it. Nest Head and me put our heads together – really – put 'em together so we could talk and not be heard.

"What should we do, Stilts?" Nest Head asked me, like I was some mastermind lawman or sumpthin'.

"We gotta make a plan," I says. "How 'bout we wake up the guys and tell 'em we're gonna capture bank robbers? That should wake 'em up in a hurry. We'd better cover their mouths while we do it so's they don't give our position away."

"Yeah!" says Nest Head, some of the tangles of his wild, curly hair fallin' into his eyes. "And we can each grab a stick, a big one, and surround them guys."

"Yeah, that's good," I agreed. "And we'll make a whole bunch of noise, like we was a hundred wild Indians and then we move in and capture them."

"Hold on," says Nest Head. "We'd better send someone for the cavalry – I mean the sheriff and Deputy Wilks first; they've got handcuffs and guns and stuff. We'll give them time to get goin' and then we swoop down on them bandits, okay?"

"Great," says I. "Who shall we send? Not Bubblubble, he's too chubby and slow. Not Ringaling, he'd come back ringin' the bell on his dang bike and give us away for sure. And Lanky Toes'd trip over them branches he calls toes "

"And Snerk's too goofy. He'd probably forget why he was goin' and end up at the candy counter. It better be Blue Eyes then. He's small but he can run like the devil was after him and he can remember stuff. Heck, he was the first one of us to learn the times tables – all of em' – right up to twelve!"

"All right," I allowed. "Let's get on about it before them robbers hightail it out of here. Boy, there's likely to be medals and such in store for us, I bet. There'll be a big writeup in the Daily Bugle too." We had to stifle our mouths then so's we didn't let out a whoop over that. I could see me walkin' around the schoolyard with a medal on my chest the next fall. I reckoned Becky Taylor'd pay attention then, you betcha.

So, we put our plan into action, just like we planned. Woke up the gang, found good sticks for weapons, (well, Snerk just took a hefty rock, but okay) and we slithered, commando-like, to six positions around those creepy bad guys. Blue Eyes was off like a rocket and as soon as Ringaling signaled us from up the tree that the sheriff's car was in sight, we was screamin' like banshees (whatever that is, but that's what Granny calls us when we get loud playin' ball). We descended on them thieves like a plague of locusts. They was just so surprised they jumped up and bumped into each other and fell down again. I think one of them peed his pants even. And here come the sheriff and deputy who trussed 'em up like Thanksgivin' turkeys and hauled their sorry butts off to jail. Oh yeah. That was the year that we was heroes! How do you like us now?

Moving On

By Carol Ritten Smith

Jason Hart knocked on the classroom door. Through the window he saw a slim young woman in a tight skirt and red heels.

She smiled at him and waved him inside. "Good afternoon, Mr. Hart. I'm Ms. Clarkson, Amy's teacher." They shook hands. "Please, have a seat." She nodded to a desk.

How many years had it been since he'd last sat in a school desk? Eighteen, anyway. He wondered if he'd fit now, tall as he was, but he managed it with no great difficulty.

Ms. Clarkson took an adjacent desk and faced him. "Thank you for coming. I'm sorry to bother you in the middle of the day."

"It's no problem. I assume this has to do with Amy?" He clasped his hands on the desk top. To his surprise they felt clammy.

"Yes. As you know we are nearing the end of the school year and the students are in the process of writing final exams."

"Right. Somehow I don't think you're going to tell me that she aced her tests, are you?" He watched her shift in her seat.

"I'm afraid not. I caught her cheating on her math exam."

Wow, he hadn't expected that. Passing notes, maybe. Or talking in class. Amy had always been a chatterbox—although lately, she'd been disturbingly silent. But to learn that she had been cheating, that felt like a kick in the teeth.

"Are you sure? She's never cheated before." Then he stopped himself. He sounded like one of those defensive parents who thinks his child is perfect. "I'm sorry. I didn't mean to question you. I'm just sort of in shock."

She nodded in understanding.

"So what happens now?" he asked. "Expulsion?"

She shook her head. "No, nothing that drastic. This is her first misdemeanour. She will receive a zero on that exam, of course, but that won't really affect her final grade. We average the marks recorded throughout the year. We feel there is too much pressure to base everything on one exam. And since we disregard the highest and lowest mark, she'll have no trouble passing into Grade Ten. She's a good student."

"A good student who cheats," he said. "So she practically gets off scot-free?"

"Not completely. I'm afraid she won't be allowed to attend the year-end camping trip."

"I wasn't aware there was one." Suddenly he felt inadequate as a parent. If Pam was alive, she would have known about it. Probably would have volunteered.

"Instead of a formal graduation ceremony, we bus the kids out to Camp Caldwell for a weekend of fun activities."

"Amy probably would have enjoyed that."

"Actually, I don't think she wanted to go. She was rather obvious with her cheating, like she hoped to get caught."

Jason closed his eyes. He could manage a busy computer software company, but one teenage girl, and he was baffled.

"Mr. Hart, I understand you lost your wife a while ago. I'm very sorry."

He glanced across at her and forced a thin smile. "Thank you. It's been hard on my kids, especially Amy. She and her mother were very close."

"I can tell she misses her greatly. Amy's not nearly as animated as when she first arrived. Fourteen is a difficult time for any girl, but for your daughter, a new school and then losing her mother, well, it's a lot for her to adjust to. I hope you don't think I'm stepping out of line, but we have a very good guidance counsellor here, Mrs. Brand. I think she might be of some help for Amy."

Surely Amy doesn't need professional help. Considering everything they'd been through, he thought his kids were adjusting well. "I'll keep Mrs. Brand in mind. Is there anything else we need to discuss?"

She stood. "No, we've covered pretty well everything."

Jason pulled himself out of the desk and unfolded his six-foot frame. "Where is Amy right now?"

"She's at the principal's office. Do you know where that is? The school is rather large."

"Not really, but I'm sure I can find it."

Ms. Clarkson smiled. "I'll walk you there."

As they zig-zagged down several corridors, he was glad she accompanied him. He looked across at her. "It's been quite a while since I had a teacher escort me to the principal's office."

She met his smile with one of her own. "Oh? Were you a frequent visitor?"

"Fairly. I skipped classes here and there. But I never cheated."

As they turned to walk down another corridor, Jason found himself distracted. If teachers had been as good looking as Ms. Clarkson when he was in high school, maybe he'd have been more motivated to stay in class.

Then he felt a sharp stab of guilt. It was the first time since Pam's death that he'd taken notice of another woman. Surely it was too soon.

Amy silently stared out the passenger side window on the drive home. When they pulled into the driveway, her hand was already on the door handle.

Jason reached across and grasped her wrist. "Hold on a minute. We need to talk."

She pulled her arm free, and sank back into the seat, her arms crossed and her eyes straight ahead.

"I'm not very happy with you right now. Cheating? Really, Amy?" Her refusal to acknowledge he was talking to her riled him and he fought to keep his temper in check. "Would you at least look at me when I'm talking to you?"

She shifted around and stared at him with cold indifference. And to think he'd hoped she might apologise or at least appear somewhat contrite. Who was he kidding? "You could have been expelled," he continued, hoping to shock her out of her complacency.

She rolled her eyes as only a teenage girl can do. "Don't be so dramatic, Dad. Cheating isn't the big deal like it used to be when you were a kid."

"You're wrong there, young lady. Cheating will always be a big deal. To prove my point, you're grounded for a week."

"Fine. Whatever." She reached for the door handle again.

"We're not done yet, so stay put!" He stretched an open hand to her.

"What?" she asked belligerently.

"Give me your cell phone."

"What? No way! Dad, it's my lifeline. I need it to keep in touch with my friends."

"It's only for a week. Besides, you'll see your friends at school. Hand it over."

With a look of pure hatred, she reached into her bag and slapped her phone into his palm. "You are being so unfair."

"Then next time, don't cheat."

She threw open the car door, jumped out, and spun to face him. "Sometimes I wish you had died instead of Mom!" Then she slammed the door hard enough to make the car rock and she stomped into the house.

Ouch! That hurt. Jason leaned back against the head rest and closed his eyes. Sitting there, he began to question himself. Had he been too hard on her? Pam probably would have handled it better. But none of their kids had ever cheated before. Not that he knew of anyway.

Life sure had a way of screwing with your plans. He never thought he'd be raising his family on his own. Without Pam at his side, he felt so darned ill-equipped to parent properly. Some days he wished he could just back away from everything, but his kids needed him, so he hung in there.

He grabbed his lap top from the backseat and headed to the house.

"Jason, wait up." Christine, his next door neighbour rushed over. She glanced about furtively before moving closer. "I didn't mean to eavesdrop, but I heard what Amy said to you," she whispered.

Wonderful. If Christine knew, everyone in the neighbourhood would soon hear about Amy's cheating.

"She's just going though a rough phase," Jason said with a wave of dismissal.

"I'm sure she didn't mean it. You know, I could talk to her. I'm very good with children."

"No. No, it's okay. We'll work it out. Thanks, anyway." Then he hurried into the house.

Zach and Trevor were smearing thick swirls of peanut butter on slices of bread when he entered the kitchen.

"What's the matter with Godzilla?" Zach asked as he dropped the knife into the wide-mouthed, plastic jar. He was only sixteen months younger than Amy, but much taller than her. Trevor, at ten, had a lot of growing yet to do.

"I'd advise you stay out of her way right now. She's grounded."

The two boys grinned at each other, and Jason knew they were planning trouble for her.

"I mean it, guys. Leave her alone. I took away her cell phone, so give her some space."

"Wow! What did she do?" Trevor asked, working his words around a mouthful of stickiness.

At first Jason thought to keep the incident private, but decided there might be a lesson to be learned here. "She cheated on a final exam."

Zach's eyes grew enormous. "No way! Amy cheated? I don't believe it."

"Well, she did, and now she's being punished. Maybe you two can learn from her mistake. Don't cheat!"

"Or at least don't get caught," Zach said. Noticing Jason was about to explode, Zach quickly added, "Just kidding, Dad. Cheating is for losers. Come on, Trev. Let's go outside and break in your new mitt."

Jason wanted to join them in a game of catch, but he had to get supper on the table. It was Kraft Dinner night.

Jason wondered who suffered most from Amy's grounding: her, the boys or himself. It was incredible how one petulant teenage girl could make an entire household miserable. But Jason stuck to his guns much to everyone's despair.

The school year ended and Ms. Clarkson was right. Amy didn't care about the missed campout. "Most of those kids are lame," she'd said.

Only three days into the summer break, Amy asked her dad if she could go to a party at a girlfriend's house that coming Friday night.

"Do I know her?" he asked, idly sorting through the mail.

"Yeah. Sherry. You drove us to the mall last month. Remember?"

He vaguely recalled dropping Amy and another girl off to shop for a few hours. The girl didn't really stand out in his mind as one to watch for trouble. "Will there be alcohol at the party?"

"Da-ad, none of us are old enough to drink."

As if that ever stopped kids, he thought. "What about boys?"

"How should I know who's invited?"

He reached for the phonebook on the counter. "What's Sherry's last name. I'll just give her parents a quick call."

Amy exploded. "Oh, forget it! One stupid little mistake and now I'm not allowed to have any fun! Thanks a lot, Dad! It's obvious you don't trust me."

"Amy, that's not it. Things can go wrong really fast at house parties."

She pounded up the stairs, halting partway to throw him a caustic look. "Why don't you just put a lock on my bedroom door and be done with it?"

If he thought he could get away with it, he'd lock her up until she was twenty-five.

Thursday evening, Jason ran into Ms. Clarkson at the gas pumps.

"Hi," he said over the hood of his black Mazda.

She drove a small hatchback, all clean and shiny and the same bright red colour as the shoes she wore the day he met her. "Oh, hi. How's your summer going so far?" she asked. She hung up the nozzle and secured the gas cap in place.

"Not bad, considering my daughter hates me."

She laughed. "Then you must be doing something right."

He shrugged. "I sure hope so. Being a single parent is tough."

"Kids can be a challenge, that's for sure." She tapped in her code. "Try not to second guess yourself. If they think you don't know what you're doing, they'll walk all over you."

"I should put you on speed dial."

She laughed lightly, retrieved her credit card as it emerged from the slot, and then opened her car door. "See you around." She waved at him as she drove away.

He smiled. There was something about her he found attractive and it wasn't just how hot she looked in her car.

Jason had the brain wave to introduce a Friday games night. The boys were on board immediately. Amy, the one he hoped to engage, if only to take her mind off the party she was missing, wasn't keen at all.

"It can be your choice," he cajoled, but she declined and headed to her room.

Trevor suggested a game of Clue. Jason figured maybe it was just as well Amy didn't want to play. Otherwise the outcome might be, Mr. Hart, killed in the living room, by dirty looks from his daughter. At least without her, he and the boys would enjoy themselves. "Clue, it is," he said, trying to ignore the thundering music coming from Amy's bedroom. Normally he would tell her to turn it down, but he decided not to poke the princess.

Saturday morning, Jason went grocery shopping while the boys were hanging out with the kid across the street, shooting hoops in his driveway. Amy had yet to get up, but hey, it was only ten-thirty. Plenty of time before the princess would arise.

Walking into the grocery store, Jason felt a bit smug. He was really getting the hang of this shopping business. He could get in, grab what he needed and be out of the store in less than fifteen minutes.

He headed straight to the frozen food section. Whoever thought to freeze pre-made meals was a genius and a godsend to single dads. The kids all loved pizza pockets, and today they were on sale. Great! He cleared out almost all they had, then moved down to the TV dinners. If his oven ever quit, they were screwed.

His cart nearly loaded, he had only one more stop: the fruit section. No cooking necessary. Turning quickly, he almost bumped into Ms. Clarkson. "Oh, hi again," he said. "I swear, I'm not stalking you," he quipped, and then noticed she seemed distraught. "Are you all right? I didn't actually hit you, did I?"

"No. No, I'm fine." She shook her head. "Actually I'm not. I just heard the news."

"What news?"

"You haven't heard? Five students were killed in a rollover last night."

"Oh, my God! That's terrible. Any of them your students?"

"The three girls." Tears pooled in her eyes.

"Let's go sit somewhere," he suggested. "How about I buy you a coffee?"

"Thank you. I could use one."

Jason flagged a stock boy working nearby and asked him to do something with the frozen food in his cart, explaining that he'd be back shortly. He guided Ms. Clarkson to the in-store café.

"How do you take your coffee?" he asked, seating her at a small table in a secluded area.

"Black, please."

He returned shortly with two coffees and a couple of muffins.

"This is very kind of you, Mr. Hart. I still can't believe it. I don't want to believe it."

"That's understandable, and please, call me Jason."

"Heather." She took a sip of coffee and set the mug down. "They were so young. Such a waste." She produced a tissue from her purse.

"What happened? Or would you rather not talk about it right now?"

"No, it's okay." She sniffed and then took a calming breath. "I guess some older boys showed up uninvited to a house party. Of course they brought alcohol with them."

Jason felt a chill run up his spine. "Weren't the parents around to chaperone?"

She shook her head. "From what I heard, they had gone to bed upstairs, and the party was in the basement. They didn't know anything was wrong until the police arrived and told them their daughter had been killed. I can't imagine their shock."

Sadly Jason could. As if it were yesterday, he clearly recalled the officer who delivered the tragic news of Pam's accidental death. He forced the painful memory aside. This recent tragedy took precedence at the moment.

"The daughter who was killed, was her name Sherry?" he asked.

"Sherry Mitchell."

Elbows propped on the table, he dropped his forehead into both palms. "Amy wanted to go to that party, but I wouldn't let her. Thank God! Who was driving?"

"One of the party crashers. I can't remember his name. I didn't know him. He was drunk and missed the curve at Turner's slough. They say the car rolled several times."

"Fool kids! You'd think by now, they'd get it, but they still drink and drive." Suddenly he felt the need to get home and hug his children close.

Jason dreaded breaking the news to Amy, but when he returned home, he couldn't find her. Zach, Trevor and the boy from across the street were playing video games downstairs.

"Do you know where Amy is?" Jason asked them.

"She said she was going to the school," Zach said, never looking up from his device.

"Yeah, she was crying. Did you take away her phone again?" asked Trevor, eyes also glued to the screen.

Jason didn't bother answering. He drove to the school and parked. Already a crowd had gathered—parents, teachers and distraught students. Bouquets of bright flowers were piling up outside the main doors. Cripes! Things like this only happened to strangers on TV, not to people they knew.

His eyes scanned the gathering. He found Amy among a group of girls, all hugging one another and weeping. Memories of Pam's funeral flashed across his mind, and for a moment all he wanted to do was get away from there. Then he saw Heather Clarkson consoling students. If she could find the courage to be there, then so could he. He got out of his car and walked over to Amy's group.

When Amy saw him, she ran to him and sobbed against his shirt while he wrapped his arms around her. He prayed for some profound words of comfort, but they never came, so he let her cry her heart out while he held her tight.

Finally she pulled back to look up at him and with tears rolling down her cheeks, said, "I could have been in that car."

"Now do you see why I wouldn't let you go?"

That made her cry even harder. "But I d...did go. I sn...snuck out my window."

Jason couldn't talk. The impact of what she'd done and the thought of what could have happened... It made him sick to his stomach.

"I'm so sorry, Daddy. But all the cool kids were going to be there. I couldn't miss it."

"Ah, Amy." He wanted to shake her and hug her at the same time.

"At first everything was good. We were having fun, visiting and dancing. And then those two guys showed up. Sherry got all drunk and stupid. I told her not to get into the car with them, but she wouldn't listen. She talked some other girls into going along, but I wouldn't."

"Thank God."

She swallowed a few sobs. "I should have begged Sherry not to go with them."

He held her face and looked her straight in the eye. "Honey, alcohol changes people. I doubt she would have listened to you."

Amy nodded. "I wish I'd never snuck out."

"It's a little too late for that now."

"I guess I'm grounded, huh?"

At the moment, he was just so thankful to have her alive, punishment hadn't crossed his mind. "We'll discuss it when we get home. Right now, you need to be with your friends. I'll wait for you by the fence."

A short while later, Amy's teacher came over to him.

"Hey, Heather," he said. "How are you holding up?" To him, she looked worn out.

She leaned back against the wire fence. "Okay. I've had training to handle situations like these, but I always hoped I'd never need to use it.

It's so hard. Everyone is devastated, but especially the girls who were at the party."

"I just found out that Amy went. She snuck out of her room. Thank God she didn't get in that car. I don't know what I'd do if I lost Amy, too. I'm not sure I could go on." He felt himself begin to shake.

Heather put a hand on his forearm. "But you would because your boys would need you. Right?" He nodded. "From what I've heard," Heather continued, "Amy was one of the few girls who refused to drink. That takes courage to stand up against her peers. And when things got really serious she knew what to do."

Jason pulled himself under control. "You're right. She did. But I can't believe she disobeyed me. I hate to admit it, but I think I'm failing my kids. Maybe they'd be better off living with Pam's parents."

Heather turned toward him. "Don't even think of it! They've lost their mother. If you send them away, it will be like they lost their dad, too. Jason, you're too hard on yourself. Even two-parent families have their problems."

"I guess so."

"And did it ever occur to you that you've had to make some major adjustments yourself? Maybe you need to talk to someone. At the very least, cut yourself some slack."

"Yeah, I maybe should do that." He gave her a smile. "You're good," he said.

"Good at what?" she asked.

"At being a shrink. Maybe you've missed your calling."

She snorted. "No way. I'm right where I want to be. I love being a teacher."

"You know what, Heather? It shows. I saw how good your are with the kids. The schools need more like you."

She pushed away from the fence. "Thanks. Knowing you feel that way helps. Now I better get back to work. Nice talking to you."

He watched her head back into the fray of upset students. He realized she was a woman he'd like to get to know on a personal level.

It was rough going to three funerals on three consecutive days, but they got through it as a family. The school opened its doors that week for any students who needed someone to talk to. Mrs. Brand, the counsellor, had been a tremendous help. Certainly, she'd helped Amy, and Jason was glad he'd encouraged his daughter to see her. He'd spent a lot of time reflecting on himself as a parent. Heather was right. He needed to relax and quit beating himself up over the decisions he made. Good or bad, he was doing his best.

One evening while he washed dishes, Amy picked up a dishtowel and began to dry the plate in the drain rack. "Thanks," he said with a smile, but he couldn't help wondering what she wanted.

"Dad," she began.

Yup, here we go, he thought.

"Do you still miss Mom?"

His hands stilled in the dishwater. He looked sideways at her. "Yes, I do. Some days more than others, but I think about her every day. Why?"

"You don't act like you do. You go on with your life just like you used to."

His heart ached hearing that. He'd been so careful to shield his kids from his grief. Maybe he'd been wrong to do that. He took the towel from Amy and led her to the table.

"Honey, how can I not think of your mother when you remind me of her every time I look at you? You have the same eyes and mouth. Same hair coloring. Same laugh even. I miss your mom a lot, but I don't get as sad as I used to when I think of her. And that's good."

Amy frowned as if his admission was a betrayal to her mother's memory.

"Sweetie, I don't want your mom to be unhappy when she looks down from Heaven, and she would be if she saw us moping around all the time. You want her to be happy, too, don't you?"

Amy nodded, tears pooling in her eyes.

"Well, I know she'd want us to move on with our lives . . . because that's exactly what I would have wanted if I had died."

Tears slid down Amy's cheek. She swiped them away with the back of her hand. "I'm really sorry that I said I wish you were dead instead of her. I didn't mean it. It's just that I miss her so much it hurts." Her lips trembled.

Jason reached out and squeezed his daughter's hand. "Ah, honey, losing someone you love is very, very hard. And each of us has to deal with it our own way. But I can tell you this: some day you'll be able to smile when you think of her and you won't feel guilty about it. I promise."

"Da-ad. The phone's for you," Zach called.

"Who is it?" he called back.

"Some lady."

Probably a telemarketer. "Okay, thanks, Zach. I've got it." He took the call in his office. "Hello?" He heard the phone in the kitchen hang up.

"Hello, Jason? This is Heather Clarkson. Amy's teacher?"

As if he wouldn't remember her. "Hello, Heather. It's nice to hear from you." He felt his heart race slightly.

"I called to see how Amy's doing."

"She's doing better. Actually quite good."

"I'm so glad to hear it."

"And what about you?" he asked. "How are you managing?"

"Well, you know what they say about good girls. You can't keep 'em down."

"Yeah, I think I've heard a country song about that."

"There's a country song for just about every situation, don't you think?"

He chuckled. "Probably. Maybe that's why I like that genre. Saves me from paying for a shrink."

She laughed again and he liked the sound of it. Then there was a pause, and he realized here was his opportunity. But it had been a good many years since he'd asked a woman out and he wasn't sure how to go about it.

"Well, I shouldn't keep you," she said, and he thought he detected a note of sadness in her voice. "I was just thinking of Amy and thought I'd call."

He gave himself a mental kick, and before he lost the nerve blurted out, "Listen, I was thinking of going to grab a coffee somewhere. Would you care to join me? That is, if you're not already seeing someone. Not that having coffee means anything, but I wouldn't want to cause you any trouble or anything." Darn it. He was making a mess of this. He should have practised what he was going to say first. "You know what? Maybe, we should just forget I—"

"I'd love to meet you for coffee, Jason."

"You would?" He cringed. "I mean, wonderful. Do you know where *Graba Java* is?"

"I love that place. They make the best Cappuccinos."

"Good. I'll meet you there in, say, half an hour?"

"Perfect."

The minute they hung up, he got busy. He needed to shower and shave. Did he have a clean shirt? Should he wear jeans or dress pants?

Fifteen minutes later, he grabbed his car keys and poked his head into the living room where the boys were watching TV and Amy was reading. Should he tell them he was taking Ms. Clarkson out for coffee? No. It was too early. Besides, it wasn't even a real date, though his knees were shaking.

"I'm going out for a bit, kids. Don't wreck the place while I'm gone."

Amy looked up from her book and said, "See you later, Dad."

And in his daughter's face, he saw Pam smile.

No Crystal Ball

By Lyle Meeres

Rosie Sandberg walked to school early, not because she needed time for lesson planning, but because it was her day for playground supervision at Ashton Elementary School. She loved her job—playground duty, not so much. Kids running unfettered sometimes did stupid things and though she tried to be on top of everything, it wasn't always possible.

Before heading for the playground, Rosie went to her classroom to drop off the materials she had taken home to work on, plus the art materials she had bought. The kids were so much fun when they got into an art project. Each child had something up on the classroom walls, but it was time for a change. The children loved to point out their newest work to friends, or if it was an open house, to parents and other relatives. Now the classroom was silent and she wanted to fill it with kids.

Rosie's mind strayed to her wish to have children of her own. Sometimes she felt that she loved her grade one students too much for her own good. She was dating Stan, a policeman, and while she cared for him a great deal, she wasn't certain yet that he would be a fabulous father. His concern that things must be right would mean that discipline would be rigid. On the other hand, he did care about people.

Rosie wasn't living with Stan, and so far she was pleased to have a bit of distance. She felt positive that it wouldn't be long until Stan suggested some kind of advancement in their relationship. She felt partially ready. Stan had lots of good qualities. She just couldn't predict the consequences of a big commitment to parenting together.

She did worry about a notion she once read, that in a relationship people are fortunate to get three or four qualities that they want in the other person. She was particularly fearful that if she waited for Mr. Right to appear, she would end up with nobody. And like her, Stan was what she would call a "moderate" personality—sensible, perhaps to an extreme. Too, Stan had passed the test: Rosie's mother approved of him.

Rosie's watch said that it was time to be on the playground so she stepped right along, past the bright displays along the walls. The cold air caught her breath when she opened the doors and stepped out. For the first bit, she walked around quickly but saw nothing troublesome.

Movement on the playground took Rosie's eyes to Bobby, one of her students. She gave him a wave. He was a sweet kid, with a fantastic imagination. At the beginning of the grade one term, it took her weeks to realize that some of his stories were just that: stories. Then when his stories got wilder, she just smiled and nodded. The one about knocking down icicles and taking one to pound on the bad guys, for example, was pretty obviously an overactive imagination creating a superhero. Rosie suggested that hitting someone with an icicle might not be a safe idea. The one about his father being a pilot in the Middle East took a parent-teacher night to become an obvious story. However, his father was a pilot so the story included a bit of truth. The whole truth, unfortunately, was that Bobby's father had died... in a car accident, of all things.

It was a cold morning. As she watched, Rosie saw Bobby wipe his nose on his coat sleeve. Just a normal kid. Bobby was headed for the swings which was a place Rosie often spotted him when she was on playground duty. With the cold, the swings wouldn't be busy this morning. Most of the children were playing games that had them running around which was a good thing since it would keep them warm.

Rosie headed for one of the groups playing a form of tag. They looked to be having a riot, seemingly unaware of the chill in the air. No problems there. She glanced back toward the swings and spotted two older boys chatting to Bobby beside the swings.

As she watched, Bobby let out a warbled shriek. He had stuck his tongue on the metal support of the swings.

Rosie made a dash for him. As she got closer, Rosie heard the two boys laugh and call out "Dummy" and "Stupid kid." They were too busy teasing to notice her approaching on the run.

Bobby had yanked his tongue off the frozen metal and was sobbing loudly, his breath coming out in little puffs of cloud.

The two boys spotted Rosie too late to avoid her grasp. She got a firm grip on each boy's jacket. "Hold it! Time to visit Mrs. Donaldson in her office."

Bobby eased back to heavy sighs. He nodded his okay to go into school with Rosie, but he glared at the metal bar framing the swings with a look of pain and distrust. A gloved hand went to his mouth. When he turned to the two boys, his attitude was predominantly astonishment.

Mrs. Donaldson was in the principal's office and for once she did not have a cluster of little people with her. "What is it Miss Sandberg?"

Rosie said, "These two boys thought it was very funny persuading Bobby to put his tongue on the frozen bars at the swings. Then when he did, they called him 'Dummy' and 'Stupid kid.'"

"There's been a bit of an epidemic of that going around. Time to make a change. I'm glad you caught these two because I suspect that they have hurt several children. I wonder how they get so many kids to go along with the notion of sticking their tongues on frozen metal."

Bobby looked up at that. "They told me that it tastes like licorice. And they double dared me to do it."

Mrs. Donaldson frowned. "I think that kind of behavior has gone on for generations. Let's try something to see if we can bring it to an end at least at this school."

Turning to the two culprits, Mrs. Donaldson said, "You boys know I don't normally use the strap, don't you?"

The comment was enough to make the two squirm. No doubt they wondered what was going to happen to them—and while it wasn't to be the strap, the uncertainty was threatening, judging by the looks of consternation on their faces.

The two looked at each other. One blurted, "I... it wasn't my idea. I just went along because Greg thought it would be fun."

"A variation on the 'I just followed orders' theme, Miss Sandberg?"

Rosie nodded. She wondered what Mrs. Donaldson had in mind for the two bullies. As a principal, Mrs. Donaldson leaned toward current approaches to discipline, and since Rosie was certain the boys had reasons for their bullying tactics, she would prefer a method that was just but not without understanding. The boys probably lacked social skills and likely faced bullying or mistreatment themselves. Still, they had to learn what was unacceptable.

"Well, I'm going to assign each of you to one month of helping the children who have been hurt by your actions. You are to report here tomorrow morning and I'll give you the details. I'm also going to notify your parents. What they do is up to them."

Mrs. Donaldson noticed that both boys reacted more to word about involving the parents than they did to the idea of helping other children. They might change their minds when they found out how long a month was. "That's all for now. Be here at first bell tomorrow morning, or I won't be so gentle. I will tell your teachers what you've done and what you are going to do about it. Go along now."

Rosie turned to her student. "You wait outside the office door for me, Bobby. I'll be along in a minute."

When the children left, Mrs. Donaldson turned to Rosie. "Tomorrow morning I'll talk to each of them separately to start them thinking about the consequences of their actions. Children have to learn that what they do affects others. I want to involve the victims, too, because they have to learn what to do if they face bullying."

Rosie nodded her agreement. "What do you think the chances are that the two boys will change their approach to others?"

"My crystal ball is on the blink, so I can't really tell. My best guess says that they are young enough to change but all the models of meanness they see in the world around them pose a risk. Let's work at change."

Rosie's feeling that she should have done more was on her mind. "I'm sorry I wasn't there in time to pour water on Bobby's tongue to make it gentler getting it off the metal, but there was no time. I'll comfort him as best I can."

It was not an isolated incident. Bullying others in order to demonstrate superiority had history on its side. Bullying would not be easy to stop.

On the way to her classroom, Rosie offered comforting words and the hope that Bobby's tongue would feel better by day's end. He nodded but walked along deep in his own thoughts.

Rosie moved into her own thoughts, too. What about Stan? In his job, Stan must face challenging situations all the time, only more severe. Children could be mean, but adults could cause real injury or death. Rosie was finding it easier to see why Stan would prefer harsh measures. She didn't like it, but she could understand. One of Stan's good qualities was that he possessed passionate fairness and a solid sense of justice. He wouldn't punish kids just to demonstrate his authority. He even had a sense of humor and parents needed that. She would likely approve of his approach to two kids like these bullies. It might be a talking point.

Those two boys might have second thoughts before they tried to intimidate other children. Rosie did what she often did: hoped for the best.

Awoken by Beauty
By Michelle T. Lambert

The evening was
calm
and I was
restless
weary
from a hard day's work
yet too tired to sleep.
Suddenly
my son burst
upon my thoughts
and dragged me
outside, my body
protesting.

Wonder of wonders!
The aurora borealis'
emerald green streamers
lit up the sky
with an intensity
I'd never imagined.

I was seized
by the moment:
thrilled
by the beauty of
cascading
movement.

The energy and beauty
of the panorama in motion
touched me
deeply
moved me
to awe
and
reverence.

I was witnessing
a vision of the divine
a picture postcard
from God.
My soul became
still and reverent
I experienced
wonderment
for all of God's creation
for all seen and unseen
for all beauty and being.

Gazing
at the intense illumination
I remembered
the words
"The Kingdom of God is
within you"
spoken to me
by a beautiful lady
in an ugly, dirty city,
many years ago.

Heaven's bowing
down
but still so high up

I couldn't get
close enough.

This beauteous event
left me with
a glimpse into
"the glory of God is
man/woman fully alive".

My body, mind and spirit
thrilled
at the sight.
It was over too soon, too quickly,
and my neck
had a crick in it.

The Would-be Knight
By Andrew Worzhak

The last star from the once proud constellation of the Owl barely shimmered at all. The rest of the Owl had blinked out one by one long ago, but this last star still struggled to make its light known amongst its brighter, stronger neighbours. Beneath this star, a young elf rushed in with his imaginary sword.

Swoosh. Kinlar imagined he was attacking a ferocious dragon. He had just sliced off half of its tail. *Dodge.* With a sharp thrust of his make-believe sword, the young elf gracefully bounced out of the way of a mouthful of phantom teeth that could chomp a house in half. *Pounce.* His elven agility propelled him gracefully into the opening under the dragon's chin where he dealt the killing blow. With the notched measuring stick as his pretend longsword held high over his head, Kinlar straightened triumphantly. No one else in the whole elven kingdom had faced the dragon, and he, Kinlar, just beat it into obscurity without becoming its next meal.

"Hey, watch wer ye bin puttin' that thing!"

The sudden croak startled Kinlar out of his fantastic victory.

"Ya near poked me hoss in the nose." The horse, a large one even for a human to use, towered over Kinlar's slight elven frame. Although, with the memory of his imaginary foe still vivid in his mind, the boy thought the huge horse could easily pass as a dragon if he only had scales.

"Sorry sir. I was just playing that I was a knight killing a dragon. I didn't mean to hurt your horse, sir. Please don't tell Master Lamron? I won't do it again."

"Don't worry lad. I ain't got no urges to see that old spook. Keep that in mind next time ya think'a killin' ma hoss, e'ain't the foul beast ye be thinkin' he be."

Kinlar let out an anxious breath, "Yes sir!" He started away at a dead run before the old farmer could say more. Someone seeing him playing a kid's game was bad enough. At 52, the adolescent elf was old enough to know better, but he'd almost hurt the man's horse and Master Lamron would've certainly been severe with the consequences.

"Where have you been, boy?" Kinlar just crossed the threshold into the tower proper when his angry Master's voice seemed to reverberate from the walls around him. "You know better than to keep me waiting. My calculations won't matter if I don't finish them in time. What was the measurement?"

Kinlar knew his pre-pubescent voice would never reach to the Master from the entrance so he ran as fast as his spindly legs could carry him through the labyrinth that was Master Lamron's tower. "14 cubits, 3 and a half palms Master," Kinlar did his best to keep his breathing measured. The wizard wouldn't forgive gasping or panting in his laboratory.

Lamron quickly jotted this information on his calculation scroll and ran it through some rather lengthy mathematical equations. "It's as I'd hoped." His Master seemed almost happy for a moment, "Kinlar, how deep was Klevar's well when he tried the summoning spell?"

"15 cubits, sir."

"Perfect! Is the webbing finished yet? It's time!"

Kinlar shrunk back. He knew what was coming. "No Master." It mattered little to Master Lamron that he had given the boy two tasks to finish at the same time and Kinlar was only one elf.

"You'd better get out there and have that webbing finished before I get there or by all that screams I will fill your head with such nightmares that you'll fear sleep for the rest of your miserable life." The blood vessels on the Master's head virtually glowed with the repressed magical energy that wanted to vaporize this useless lump of fairy dust.

Kinlar didn't wait around to listen to the rest of his owner's tirade. He bolted toward the inner courtyard of the tower at such a speed that he felt, for a moment, as though he were flying. Lucky for him, Kinlar had managed to scrape together enough understanding from his Master's notes that he had learned a couple of rudimentary spells. He could use one for weaving the intricate web of caterpillar silk.

Lamron marched out into the courtyard just as the spell finished the last few strands of the web.

"Move boy!" Kinlar wasn't sure if his body moved by his own muscles or by the magical energy in his master's voice. "Leave me and go clean the library. I'll be at this for a while and I want my library cleansed of all its dusty contamination when I get there."

A shout jolted him out of his restful slumber and dreams of righteous conquest. "Kinlar! Where are you, you diseased pile of rat droppings. I've had some news and need to travel right away."

Kinlar had just time enough to rub the sleep from his eyes and stand when the door to the library burst open from the force of a charging bear. Master Lamron looked like an overweight arms master. His jaw and knuckles were tightly muscled while his belt line embraced more girth than any fit man would allow. He wore a functional woolen tunic and breeches that had certainly seen happier days. There was, about his face, a look of constant disappointed ambition. "There you are, boy. Come, help me pack."

Excitement surged through Kinlar like the electricity from a lightning bolt through an armor-clad knight. "Where are we going, sir?"

"*We* are not going anywhere, boy. *I* am going to see an old friend who has had a little trouble and has requested my help. The situation is touchy enough that I must go alone." Kinlar was only a little disappointed at not going. He dared hope Master Lamron would let him stay at home. The spark of hope faded, however, with Lamron's next words. "Old Quodley at the Wastrel Inn will likely be able to use another hand for a time while I'm away."

Kinlar didn't know much about 'Old Quodley', but the idea of living somewhere other than Master Lamron's tower was the most frightening idea he could imagine. The dragons in the stories he had read weren't as scary. That a stranger would be telling him what to do and where to sleep was terrifying. But, the worst was that he would be ruled by a very different set of rules. Master Lamron may be quite strict and quick with the punishment, but at least Kinlar could predict his reactions. He wanted to beg Master Lamron to let him stay, but remembered that the desires of a slave were worth very little to his owner.

Master Lamron had only just departed, leaving Kinlar at the inn. He left little in the way of instructions with the inn keeper other than: "keep the boy out of trouble". Quodley looked Kinlar up and down with a sharp frown. "What am I going to do with you? You don't look like you could even lift a pot." His voice contained the familiar tone of angry contempt when he spoke to his new charge.

The young elf knew the innkeeper wasn't expecting an answer, so he just stood there looking at his feet. "Why don't you just scrub the floor. You know how to do that don't you?"

"Yes sir."

"Good, the wash bin is over in the corner," he waved his hand vaguely behind the youth.

Kinlar spent the rest of the day and night cleaning up food and grime without pause or complaint. Several times Quodley kicked Kinlar in the face or gut when the boy didn't move out of the way fast enough. It didn't take long for the agile young elf to learn to anticipate his substitute Master's movements and be somewhere else before the man got there.

Kinlar sat awake in the small room at the back of the inn's attic. He didn't understand how to deal with this new twist he'd been handed. At home, he always had a sense of purpose. His errands here at the inn seemed less important than the forgotten room he had been pushed into when Quodley had finally decided to let the underfed boy have some rest. He had dismissed Kinlar less than two hours before dawn with instructions to get some rest and be in the kitchen for the morning meal.

He looked up from his brooding to find the sun just cresting the horizon. He wondered if Quodley would mind if he took a walk in the fresh air to calm his thoughts. He likely would. This man was not Kinlar's Master though, so he decided that it didn't matter what this new slave driver wanted.

The early air was cool. The village was still quiet in its preparations for the coming day. The elf, relieved to see that there was nobody around, climbed down from his tiny attic window. A movement caught his eye as he turned up the street. He tip-toed over and observed something close to pure grace.

A man moved in some sort of slow motion dance. Kinlar didn't know humans could be so graceful. He wore loose cotton breeches tied with a length of coarse rope. The muscles of his chest and arms held tense like a leopard about to pounce. His skin glowed with exertion. His motion reminded Kinlar of a cross between a panther's deadly elegance and a blacksmith's precise placement. Even the slight morning breeze seemed to be a part of the dance.

Those movements so engaged Kinlar's attention that he didn't notice when the man looked at him. "Can I help you son?" His voice sounded like rolling thunder. The boy stood transfixed by this image that so completely contradicted his own experience of what men from this part of the world looked like. "Son?"

Kinlar jolted into the moment. The man's voice was like the sounds of soft snow thundering down the side of Mount Paradise. "Sorry sir. I was just out for a walk and saw your dance. It was... enchanting. I've never seen anything like it. I wish I knew how to do that?"

"It takes a lot of discipline, as well as time and practice. Are you a fighting man, boy?" The stranger's demeanor was just as alien as his physical image. The gentleness Kinlar heard in this man's tone caused him to doubt all he knew of men.

Suspicious of such kindness, Kinlar hesitated. "No sir. I just run errands for Master Lamron."

"Come on over here and let me have a look at you. Let's see what you're made of." Kinlar didn't have the ability to disobey a direct request so he cautiously stepped closer. The man looked Kinlar over like some of Lamron's associates had, but this time he didn't feel like live stock under the scrutiny.

"You're a little skinny, and quite gangly, but so are most elves in my experience. Here, show me what you can do with this." He handed

75

Kinlar a practice sword from a table behind him where it lay amongst a variety of other weapons.

Kinlar took the weapon with some trepidation. After a moment to orient himself and gather his courage, he tried to remember the movements described in the adventure stories he'd read about. He turned and imagined that there was a soldier facing him. He imagined a fierce battle around him. The soldier became a king in full battle dress. He had to kill the king to save the world from an iron fisted tyranny. Kinlar went through the moves that he imagined would best the king; the man behind him watched with interest. When Kinlar shouted with his killing thrust finishing his fantasy. He came abruptly back to the ordinary yard, suddenly dropping the wooden sword where he stood. He felt embarrassed and waited to be punished for daydreaming.

"That was very good. I thought you said you weren't a fighting man. What you just did would have bested a lot of experienced swordsmen. Where did you learn to do those things?" Kinlar didn't understand the sincerity in the man's tone and demeanor.

"Out of stories, sir. I just paid special attention to the descriptions of the battles and tried my best to copy them."

"That explains the lack of balance and apparent clumsiness of your style. Well, it seems I have a lot more to work with than I thought. I might be able to teach you that 'dance' if you'd like." He started gathering up his practice weapons. "My name is Tompsle and I'd like to see what you can do with a little coaching. It'll have to be another time though; I smell breakfast cooking and I'm hungry."

Kinlar looked up and saw that the sun was well up over the horizon now. Instinctively, he turned and bolted toward the kitchen, his body tensing for the beating he could already feel.

It was hard, but Kinlar found his training with Tompsle was much less exhausting than the work he did at the inn. He and his coach met earlier in the mornings so he could still be in the kitchen before breakfast. The beatings he got when Quodley became frustrated at something usually not Kinlar's fault started to hurt less as Kinlar learned how to center himself to reduce the effect; though his frail elven body held the bruises for days. After a while, he started using some of the balancing techniques in his work. He found it made most of his tasks easier to do. He even started to treat his chores as tests of his progress. At first it mostly just took the strain off the wrong muscles and put it on the ones best suited to the work. After a while, though, he started using his imagination with these new techniques to make things quicker. The basic spell casting he knew from his Master's library also helped when nobody was around. The things he learned from Tompsle showed him many ways of doing things that he would never have dreamed of without the training. Soon Kinlar finished earlier each time and he managed to escape to visit Tompsle in the evenings as well.

Master Lamron had been gone for two weeks and Kinlar was beginning to enjoy his visit to the village. The work at the inn wasn't so bad after all and Tompsle had started teaching him to use a sword. In fact, just this morning, Tompsle had hinted that he might have someone for Kinlar to spar with this evening. Kinlar didn't even bother to wash himself off after scrubbing the stables all afternoon. He ran straight over to see what Tompsle had lined up for his evening lesson.

Kinlar stopped dead in his tracks when he rounded the corner and saw who Tompsle was talking to. He was the biggest brawl stopper Quodley had in his employ. The huge man towered over Kinlar by a foot and a half and weighed at least double the elf's slight frame. The bladed weapon that hung from a shoulder strap looked more like the mighty sword used by the gods themselves than anything a mere mortal could wield effectively. Kinlar knew better though. He'd watched this man use that sword to deadly effect one evening when a pair of mercenaries had thought to carve their way out of paying their bill.

"This is Tictor," Tompsle introduced, "He and his sons help when someone teaches young men to fight. He has agreed to let one of them spar with you to show us how much you have learned."

Tompsle stepped aside to let a youth come forward. Tictor's son couldn't have been more than 14 years old, but he was almost as huge as his father. At least the sword he carried strapped to his belt was easier to imagine in human hands. "This is my son, Tito," Tictor said.

Kinlar was suddenly less sure of his new skills. "Sir, I don't think I've prepared enough to train with a living opponent."

Tito sniffed. "What's the matter, manure man? Scared to spar with the real men?"

His voice reminded Kinlar of the girls that served Quodley's patrons; high pitched with more than a hint of tease. The elven youth turned to hide his face or risk letting his humor show.

"Don't go running away just yet little one." Tictor thankfully misunderstood Kinlar's expression, "My son is well trained and will be easy on you until you get used to fighting a live opponent."

Grateful for the distraction, Kinlar turned to consider his adversary. The punishment he could receive from this young warrior couldn't be any worse than the beatings he'd been getting from Quodley. The experience would be quite valuable, however. He decided to see if he actually could hold up against a trained fighter.

Tompsle handed Kinlar a short wooden practice sword as the young elf deliberated. The slave boy looked at it, trying, without much success, to gain some confidence from the pretend weapon. After a moment, he took it and conditioned himself to its weight as the two men moved farther back to give the combatants room to maneuver. He looked over to see his rival had removed his belt and sword and now held a practice sword half again the size of his own.

Kinlar waited, hoping his warrior instincts would take over. He saw the other boy's weapon close in on his sword arm. In less time than it would take to position his sword for the block, he analyzed, calculated, and quickly hopped backward. The tip of his opponent's wooden sword snagged and ripped the elf's tunic but missed everything else. He considered taking it off, but the thought of letting anyone see his frail body made him feel violated.

Tito was obviously surprised that his attack could be so easily avoided. His brow furled in concentration. Kinlar simply watched and waited. The next assault was aimed at his head. Kinlar started to duck but decided to jump and felt the air whistle under his feet. The large boy growled when his feint met with success identical to his first attack.

Kinlar tired of waiting for these battle instincts that were so important to the heroes he read about. He decided to use a little wit and imagination to overcome the younger swordsman. He waited for Tito to launch his next attack. When it came in the form of a diagonal slash at the shoulder, his elven reflexes brought up his own sword to deflect the attack over his head while he leaned his upper body backward and brought his foot to bear on the boy's chin. The youth was large and steady, but obviously not well centered since Kinlar's kick knocked him on his back.

Like a sudden thunderstorm, the young fighter jumped up and ran at Kinlar yelling like a maniac. Kinlar saw no alternative other than to defend himself. He dove aside into a roll and threw his sword at the boy's legs.

When the charging Tito's feet became entangled in the sword, he landed on his face in the dirt. The men came running over to prevent what was quickly becoming a brawl where one fighter would have to kill the other or be killed.

Tictor grinned down at his son, "All right boy, get a hold of yourself before you hurt somebody."

Tictor reminded Kinlar of a minotaur, but the one from children's tails that laughed too easily.

"Let the lesson here show you that brute force will only get you killed in a real fight. Let's go have an ale to sooth your injured pride." The big man said as he picked up his son more to prevent him from charging into the attack again than because he needed help.

Tompsle watched the father not so gently guide his son toward the tavern. "Pretty good for your first opponent, although I would've liked to see how you could do with your sword as a weapon," he looked at Kinlar. "You showed great balance and good reactions, but sometimes a charging bull isn't so easy to avoid."

Kinlar missed his morning lesson the next day. Quodley had woke him out of bed much too early to meet with Tompsle. The elf grunted with the effort of lifting the fork loaded with horse dung. The stiffness was finally working out of his muscles after the long day's work in the stables. The night before had produced only painful restless sleep. The adolescent growing pains that often kept him awake nights were quadrupled after being tightly tensed during his mock battle with the other boy.

Less stiffness let him almost welcome the menial work. The only difficulty he had to worry about now was the stamina that little food and less sleep had left him lacking. He found it quite easy, however, to forget his physical obstacles when he thought about what his training and a little imagination had allowed him to do to a trained warrior. Kinlar had rarely felt the satisfaction of accomplishment, and never in a physical sense.

Quodley's repulsive voice interrupted his private happiness as he reveled in his victory. "Wizard's boy, get your scrawny little ass over here. You have a visitor of great importance who isn't to be kept waiting."

Kinlar looked up from his work, his contempt for the fat innkeeper clearly etched into his features. "I'll be out as soon as I wash my hands."

The slave boy felt like he talked to himself since Quodley had already turned and walked away without waiting for a response. He glanced at the empty doorway before walking over to the water trough to scrub his face and hands. Satisfied that his touch wouldn't invite some rotting disease, he ran his hands roughly though his hair to give it some semblance of order and went out to meet his 'important visitor'.

He was happily surprised when he walked out of the stable to see Tompsle standing a few feet from the doorway. "Are you the one looking for me?" Kinlar sounded almost hopeful.

"I have something to show you and have paid Master Quodley so I could have you to myself for the rest of the day." Looking around to be sure the inn keeper didn't stick around, he added in a lower tone, "I would ask first that you join me for lunch at my humble abode."

Kinlar, caught between his two strongest motivations – curiosity and hunger, didn't argue, but followed Tompsle who apparently already had an agenda. Without a second thought for the work he would have to finish tomorrow, he stepped quickly to walk beside his mentor.

Tompsle's home did indeed look humble. It consisted of a grain shack attached to what must have been a blacksmith's forge before Tompsle's occupation changed the feel of the place more to a military bunk than a profitable business. To the forge area Tompsle had added a three-legged table and a couple of stools. The walls were still covered with the tools of a blacksmith and the furnace still housed the only source of heat. The workbench on the far wall where the blacksmith crafted the nonmetal parts of his wares displayed Tompsle's few household possessions. Where had once been a gate-like door to allow the passage of carts was now just a curtain, probably to his bedroom in the grain shack. There was nothing cozy about the dwelling, but it was functional and clean. It seemed like a place someone would rest himself and his possessions until he moved on to another life.

"I said it was humble." Tompsle looked none less proud of his custom made home. His gaze went around the room with a fatherly admiration. "It is not the prettiest place to hang my hat, but it is comfortable."

He busied himself for a few minutes gathering and preparing a meal. Kinlar thought it would be more appropriate in the home of some royalty rather than a simple solitary man like Tompsle. When he finished, Tompsle motioned for Kinlar to sit on one of the stools and took the other at the opposite side of the table. After a simple benediction, the host motioned for Kinlar to serve himself.

Tompsle spoke up after swallowing a juicy cherry tomato, "You have been progressing rapidly through your training and I wanted to reward you for your quick learning." He popped the bees wax off of a clay jar that made Kinlar think of Master Lamron's laboratory. "However, before I give you your prize, I wanted to ask if you have any plans for using what I have taught you. We have reached a point were those plans would have a bearing on what I teach you from here on through."

Caught with his mouth full of a delicious roast duck, the boy took the time to think about a question he had never considered before. "I've never thought about it because I am usually too busy doing my Master's bidding to give any thought to what I might want for myself." In truth, he did want his freedom, but he was Lamron's slave and his Master wasn't about to set him free. The meal before him only served to accent how much differently Tompsle treated Kinlar than his Master did. "Maybe if you taught me to use this 'dance' to improve my performance in my regular duties, I would have time to think about what I might want to become once Master Lamron has used up his need of me." Kinlar knew that Master Lamron would die someday while the elf was still young in elven terms, but he firmly believed his Master would have some devious plan for his slave when that time came. Tompsle's question made him wish for more.

Tompsle considered for a moment while he spooned some strawberry preserves onto Kinlar's plate. "In that case I will show you better concentration and how to access your ingenuity. That will mean it would likely be quite a while until you need this, but I will present it to you as a future reminder of what will come when you feel the need for battle awareness." As he spoke, he pulled from the bottom of the table where a sheath must have been fastened, an amazingly crafted sword that seemed to be built exactly for Kinlar's proportions. It looked plain, but Kinlar had seen what kind of quality Master Lamron demanded when someone wanted him to enchant a blade with magical properties. This weapon was one of the finest.

He sat stunned into silence for a moment. "Why would you want to give that away. It must be worth an enormous fortune." His elven eyes recognized the color of the steel and precision of the edge. "I, certainly, am not worthy of such a gift. There must be somebody who could use this much better than I could." Kinlar shied away from the perfection and … the honor? To accept a gift like this was to accept the responsibility that goes with it. He had never imagined himself as someone with value, or honor. Did Tompsle honestly believe his student was worthy of this blade? How could he?

Tompsle answered without pause. "Why I give this to you is for me to know. Someday you may understand my reasons better, but for now please just take this sword and remember all that I have taught you."

Kinlar never got the chance to find out what useless chores Quodley might drum up as revenge for his absence from the innkeeper's presence. He stopped short when he entered the inn, surprise and fear battling for control of his facial muscles. There, getting a very unflattering report from Quodley, stood Master Lamron.

The slave boy wavered with the emotions that nearly toppled him as he suddenly realized all that Lamron's appearance meant. Only his new abilities gave him the strength to control his outward expression. Fear and regret battled with loneliness and relief. He'd missed the security of his home in his Master's tower, but going home meant the end of his time with Tompsle. It also meant he would never again see the sword he'd left in Tompsle's care. For the first time in his life, Kinlar wanted something more than his freedom. Only he couldn't figure out if he would miss Tompsle more, or his new sword.

The Magician's Daughter

By Lyle Meeres

One day long ago in a land inhabited by dragons, damsels in distress, knights in armor, and teddy bears, there grew a charming little daughter named Gabriela. Gabriela was the sweetness and light in the lives of Helen, a lady not in distress, and Marvel, who called himself a conjurer though the king called him a sorcerer, and you might call him a magician. Helen called him a trickster. When she learned to talk, Gabriela called him Daddy.

Gabriela was Marvel's weakness. Where other fathers might come home from work and growl at their children, Marvel could deny his daughter nothing.

Now you might expect that this would turn her into a spoiled child. It did not. In fact, Gabriela developed an inner nature to match her pleasant, friendly appearance. Indeed, it was said that Gabriela's smile could charm an angry dog because her smile was not just an appearance. She really did love all of life.

Now at times, the Lady Helen would worry that her well-meaning husband would spoil their daughter. Indeed, she had a plan to make Marvel's love harmless, but she could not put her plan into action right away, so she watched and did what she could to keep Gabriela delightful inside as well as out.

As Gabriela grew old enough to walk and talk, she became a very loving person. She had so much love that she gave it freely to all, even the most ugly frogs, and her love only grew. Lady Helen got frown lines on her face when she read stories to Gabriela, and Gabriela said things like, "The trolls weren't really bad, Mommy." Another time she said, "I would love Cinderella's sisters. Then they would be nice."

When there was nothing else to give her love, usually at bedtime after her candle had been blown out, Gabriela turned to Bruin, her faithful teddy bear. Though his fur became a little worn and Helen had to sew his left arm back on, Bruin was the best-loved teddy bear in all the land.

And he was worth the care and attention, for through the most difficult of teddy bear days, Bruin just smiled. And when Marvel was home, Gabriela loved to watch the way her father could take coins from Bruin's ears and pretty red and blue scarves from Bruin's mouth.

Now it happened that one day when Lady Helen, Marvel, Gabriela, and of course Bruin, were out for a walk, on the edge of a mountain they came to a dark cave.

In the mouth of the cave was a very large, very fearsome dragon, with an enormous spiked tail that thrashed back and forth. In front of the dragon was a damsel, lying on the ground, her hair in disarray, and she was calling out for help.

Just out of reach of the dragon was a knight who was indeed a dashing figure. He would dash left and flames from the dragon's fierce snout would follow him. The knight would dash right, and flames would follow him. He would dash back, out of reach, and the dragon seemed to smile.

Now one thing was odd, and it was this. Marvel the Magician did not appear to watch the horrifying scene before them. Indeed, his eyes were on Gabriela.

For the first time in her young life, Gabriela had a problem. Her young heart reached out to the damsel, and to the dashing knight. But the dragon was just too much.

Gabriela watched the knight's futile efforts as he dashed right and left, back and forth, and flames followed his every path. The dragon would not leave the damsel to chase the knight, nor could the knight get past the dragon to save the damsel. Try as he might, the knight was blocked by flames. Even his shining armor looked singed here and there where the flames had come close.

Gabriela could see that the knight was trying and trying to get closer, but all that happened was his armor became more and more blackened. And he seemed to dash a little more slowly. Indeed, it appeared that one dash soon would be the knight's last, for the fearsome flames more and more often danced on the armor of the knight.

Gabriela could not love the dragon.

Finally, with Bruin drooping to the ground and Gabriela's mouth turning downward in a way it never had before, her tearful eyes asked her father to do one more thing for her.

Marvel lifted an arm and gestured toward the cave. The knight shouted, and when Gabriela turned to look again at the scene of horror, the dragon was gone and the knight was lifting the damsel into his arms.

While Gabriela watched in fascination, the knight carried the damsel to his horse and the two of them rode off. Just before they passed into the forest, the knight turned and lifted his shield in recognition to Marvel, who smiled and looked at his daughter.

"Well, would you look at that," Marvel said, taking a soft plush rabbit from under Bruin's right foot. "I'm sure Bruin wanted you to have this," and Marvel gave the cheerful-looking bunny to Gabriela who hugged it close and smiled her biggest smile.

"Now, dear, would you like to know how I did that?" Marvel asked Gabriela.

Gabriela just looked puzzled.

Lady Helen took her husband's arm and said firmly, "Dear, I think it's time we talked about some magic that I have in mind..." And the family walked back to their comfortable little home near the castle.

The dragon never reappeared, though Marvel swore that the dragon's magic allowed him to change his form.

And whenever Marvel would ask Gabriela if she wanted to know how he did his magic, she always replied, "No."

She did, however, one day ask where her little brother came from.

Old Dog, New Tricks

By Jenna Hanger

As soon as Allan Brigley walked through the door, he knew he was in trouble. There were the obvious signs: Bonnie Raitt's more sorrowful tunes seeping through the speakers, no smell of supper sweetening the air. Then there was the less-than-subtle sign, Nora's grey suitcase sitting on the landing.

Al stood in the doorway, clutching the doorknob, the cool spring air playing pleasantly on his back, a nice contrast to the stifling heat in the house. He had long since relinquished the fight over the thermostat, contenting himself to turn it down at night and keep the living room window cracked just the slightest. He shifted his weight debating the merits of quietly backing out and postponing whatever lay ahead. He eyed the suitcase again trying, to decide how serious it was. Nora had packed a suitcase four times in their sixty-one years of marriage. She left once though, for about an hour before she came back. That was usually how things went. If Al stayed quiet enough during a fight, the storm would eventually pass. She would often turn and stomp away, her little frame vibrating with anger. After a few minutes Al would go after her, offer an apology, which she would wave away saying it was her fault, she overreacted, sorry for being so dramatic and then that would be that. Still it was better to get it over with now than later, but what on earth was it? Did he do something wrong? She had seemed distant the last few days; he figured a fight was coming, but not a Bonnie Raitt level, certainly not a "no supper" one and definitely not a suitcase worth. What the hell had he done?

"Nora?" He stepped more fully into the house, shut the door and squared his shoulders. "Honey?"

Nora came down the stairs, her hair flowing in soft grey curls around her flushed cheeks.

Al motioned to the suitcase, "What's this then?"

"I'm going to visit Ellen."

"You're going to Montreal? When did you decide this?"

"Today."

"Shouldn't we talk about it?"

"No."

"No?"

"You would tell me not to."

"Why would I tell you not to go to your sister's?"

"You wouldn't say, 'Don't go'. You would say, 'Let's think about it for a while,' which just means no."

"Well, we should think about it before we just go on a trip."

"It's not 'we' it's me. I'm going. You don't like going."

"No, but I would go if you wanted me to."

"I don't want to go with someone who doesn't want to go. It will wreck the trip."

"I've come to Ellen's before. I don't think I wrecked it then."

"Yes, but after I get to Ellen's, she and I are going to New York."

"New York? Why in the hell are you doing that? Just the two of you?"

"Yes."

"You can't do that!"

"Yes I can!" Ellen raised her chin defiantly. "I am turning seventy-six this year, Al, seventy-six! Things are going to start slowing down a lot faster, and I have things I want to do still!"

"Okay...okay, yes, but you don't want to do those things with me?"

"I have tried to do things with you for sixty years."

"That's not..."

"True? Yes, it is," Nora said. "I'm tired of waiting for you to decide you're ready to do things. And I'm even more tired of forcing you. It's not fun when I know you don't want to."

Al shook his head, a sick feeling starting to grow in the pit of his stomach. "So you're just going to take off? Leave your boring husband behind?"

"Don't be like that."

"How else should I be?"

"Al, stop."

"Stop what?"

"Talking to me like I'm a child who hasn't thought things through."

"I'm not! But if you just decided today, you can't have thought it through that much, Nora."

"I've been thinking about it for a while now."

"But you never thought to talk about it?"

"We're talking now!"

Al sighed, he was going to get nowhere with her now. She was in her battle stance, hands on her hips and her special pissed-off look taking over her features. It used to make him laugh in his younger, naïve days, which never helped. He had never met anyone who could scowl like she did though. Her eyes would turn to slits, her brows came together in a deep furrow, causing a wrinkle to appear between them, and her mouth would become slightly pinched. Then she would just stare, daring him to say something, so she could throw it right back at him. He leaned against the door and waited. Letting Nora's chosen soundtrack fill the silence.

I can't make you love me, if you dooooooon't. I can't make your heart feel something it wooooon't. Here in the darkkkkk, these final hours...

"Are you going to say anything?" Nora demanded.

All right, a battle it will be. "How are you and Ellen going to manage in New York? Neither of you have ever been. Do you have any idea how big New York is?"

"We will be fine."

"Ellen is too scared to go to the mall by herself. And you get lost coming home from visiting the grandkids. How the hell will you be fine?"

Nora turned on her heel and stalked away. Al kicked off his shoes and followed her to the kitchen. "Nora, come on, this is ridiculous!"

"It's not!" She whirled to face him. "It's not ridiculous! You may be a stubborn man who is content never doing anything, but I am not! I don't want have a long list of things I never did when I'm sitting in the nursing home, losing my marbles."

"I don't do anything?"

"You're just content, never wanting anything, never experiencing new things. You might as well roll into your grave!"

Al stared at her for a minute, not saying a word. She held his gaze at first, then looked away. "Well, that would make things easier for you wouldn't it," he said quietly.

"Al..."

"When are you leaving?"

"I didn't mean..."

He put his hand out, stopping her. "I'm going for a walk." He turned and slowly walked back to the porch, grabbed the shoehorn to help slip his feet into his runners and stepped out of the house. He paused for a minute, trying to decide which direction to go, finally settling on the street leading to downtown, and set off. She didn't want him gone. He knew that. It was all the damn funerals they had been to lately; it seemed every second weekend there was another one. It's got her all in a panic, makes her think the world is gonna end tomorrow. She probably wouldn't go, he decided. She liked to act tough, but when it came down to it she had a lot of great ideas, but never really finished anything she started. It's the same reason she flitted from job to job and started one hobby with a passion, only to let it dwindle out and start a new one. No, this idea would fade. He would be damned if he'd let Ellen and her go off on their own to New York. Common sense and direction were not strong traits of the sisters, and together they seemed to be worse.

Yet this wasn't the first time something like this had come up, Nora wanting to do something crazy and complaining about him being boring. In fact it was just the latest of many over the years. He remembered one specific moment early on in their marriage. Once—they must have been late twenties by then—they decided to go out to a movie leaving the twins with a babysitter. On the way home they stopped by the lake to go for a walk, one of their favorite ways to end a date. They walked on the dock in companionable silence, the wood creaking beneath their feet, swaying slightly with the water moving underneath. The sun was just beginning to set, casting an orange and pink glow in the sky. The few clouds in the horizon had a purplish hue, making the whole thing look like an artist's masterpiece. It would have been a very nice moment, if not for Nora suggesting they try skinny-dipping. She mentioned it half-jokingly, but with the look in her eye that said she would do it. He said something about "never doing that in a million years," which sparked something in her leading to a hostile argument about being no fun, why not live on the edge a little and so on. He came back with how they had kids and needed to be responsible. She said something about how the fun had ended, how, before they had kids, they never did anything exciting. That was the end of the evening. He didn't think it was a big deal and shrugged it off, but she had been mad the rest of the night.

Al shoved his hands in his pockets looking but not seeing the displays in the shop windows. Maybe he wasn't the most exciting guy around, but he didn't find a thing wrong with not wanting to get nude in a public place, or not wanting to jet off to New York at a moment's notice for that matter.

His stomach rumbled loudly, voicing its annoyance with Nora's chosen time to start a fight. He patted it in sympathy, thinking he better turn back to see what leftovers were in the fridge when a sign on the window across the street caught his eye. 'BREAKFAST SERVED ALL DAY'. He bit the inside of his cheek considering, then made his way across the street. He had never been to this café before, but had walked by it a few times. Breakfast was his favorite meal and would be better than leftovers. A blast of warm air engulfed him as he entered, making him shiver as he left the brisk air outside. He didn't realize how cold it had gotten with the sun dipping down. The smell of fresh coffee was strong and reassured him he made a good decision. A cup would definitely be good right about now.

It was a small diner, a dozen or so booths which all looked the same, green cushions matching green tables. The walls were brown with local art hanging above each table. There seemed to be only one waitress working, a young girl with her brown hair drawn up in a messy bun. She wore jeans and a black t-shirt with a red apron tied securely around her hips. She came towards him, holding a tray balancing three plates full of eggs, bacon and hash browns.

"Hi there!" she said pausing. "You can sit yourself down anywhere, or are you waiting for someone?" She peered around him to see.

Al felt his face flush, suddenly feeling nervous. "No, no it's just me."

She smiled, a little sympathetically, Al thought.

"Well pick wherever, I'll be there in a minute to take your order."

Only four tables were already taken. Al quickly surveyed the room, his eyes latching on to an empty booth in the back corner. He made his way there, trying to ignore the feeling people were watching him. He had never eaten out alone before. He always thought there were two types of people who went to a restaurant alone: the first, an extremely confident person who was very secure and didn't mind a little alone time; the second, a sad and lonely human who couldn't find anyone willing to come. He hoped he came across as the first. Though he supposed there was a third type now, those who were too scared to go home and argue with their wife again.

The waitress came a few minutes later and handed him a menu. He asked for a cup of coffee–decaf, black—after she left, he flipped open the menu. His gaze immediately sought the prices before any of the tempting pictures. If Nora was wondering where he was, she'd certainly never guess eating out. She often complained about having to beg to go out to eat, and then when he finally consented, how he would make her feel guilty for ordering anything other than water. He would say it was bloody expensive, and better it be more of a treat instead of a habit, to which an eye rolling was usually given in reply.

"Well, here I am now Nora, pretty spontaneous I would say," he muttered.

"Sir? Your coffee?"

Al started, then cleared his throat, sure his face was glowing. How long had she been standing there? She smiled kindly at him, probably assuming she was serving some senile old man.

"Are you ready to order?" She reached across the table and filled the waiting mug with the pot in her hand.

"Yes, I will have strawberry pancakes with sausage, please."

She nodded, then took his menu and moved on to offer the next table refills. Now what? He wished he had a newspaper or something to make himself look busy. Al wrapped his hand around the warm handle of the mug and brought the coffee to his lips, taking the tiniest sip of the steaming bitter drink and enjoying the taste filling his mouth. He then snuck a look at the tables around him. There was a family sitting near the front with three small children—probably all under the age of five—yapping like pups, jumping up and down, poking and prodding each other. Their parents looked appropriately exhausted, past the point of trying to tame them and stared blank-eyed at the menus. Directly across from him, there was a couple, both tapping madly away on their phones. Of course, people can't even sit through a meal without being on those things. In fact, looking around, most people had their heads bent over their devices. Nora loved her cell phone. She texted more than she called anyone now. He never got what the big deal was with them and felt irritated whenever he saw her on it. He shook his head, taking another sip. He was starting to feel a little more relaxed as he realized people were too wrapped up in their own worlds to give him a second thought. Sooner than he expected the waitress came around. She set down a plate full of gleaming red berries on whipped cream, smothered over three generous pancakes. Four sausages clung to the edge of plate. Their aroma made his mouth water in anticipation. No way could he finish all this, but it wouldn't be from lack of trying. He eagerly picked up his fork, and for a few moments, didn't think of anything but the food in front of him. When he was done he sat back, satisfied and in a much better mood.

"How is it tasting?" The waitress asked, coming up with the pot of coffee in hand.

"It was great, I am afraid I can't finish it all."

"Would you like a box?"

"No, I am fine, thanks, I might take a little more coffee though."

"'Course." She tipped more coffee into his mug. "Let me know if you need anything else."

After she walked away, Al yawned and checked his watch. He had been gone for almost an hour. He better get back soon or he would miss the window between Nora apologizing and being pissed because he wasn't home yet. Al leaned forward to fish his wallet out of his back pocket. Hopefully, by the time he got back, that damn suitcase would be gone and...His thoughts got cut off as his fingers reached into his pocket. His empty back pocket. He checked the other side, then his coat pockets, a feeling of panic tightening his chest. Where was it? He couldn't have left without it, could he? He checked under the table and slid his hands in the crack in the booth in desperation. This never happened to him, ever. Now what? He glanced around, briefly making eye contact with the man across from him. Should he ask to borrow some money? No, he couldn't. He would come across as a forgetful old man who should be in a home or something. Ask to come back and pay? See if he could borrow someone's damn phone and call Nora?

"How's it going, sir? Do you want anything else?" The waitress startled him, making him jerk his cup and splash coffee on the table.

"S-sorry, no I... Actually I...I am just gonna sit for a little if that is all right." Coward.

"Of course! I'll meet you at the front when you're ready to pay." She wiped up the spill with a napkin, then turned to greet the guests who just entered.

Al's heart was beating painfully against his ribcage. What on earth was he going to do? There weren't many good options. He could run, make a break for it. The thought sent a tremor through his body, adrenaline and pure terror probably. He had never in his life stolen anything before, or broken any major rules. Nora's words echoed back to him, boring, predictable, safe. Well, we will see about that. Stuffing his trembling fingers into his front pockets, Al watched the waitress take the newcomers orders and disappear to the back. Now or never. He got up slowly, moving at what he hoped was a casual pace. No one seemed to be watching him, but he felt like a million eyes were searing the back of his skull. He took one step, then another, trying his best to look like an innocent old man. If he got caught, he would just pretend he thought he paid, or forgot where he was. They would probably buy that. Would they still call the cops? He made it to the door without anyone stopping him. One more quick look around, then he pushed the door open and slipped out. He turned and hurried as fast as his old legs would carry him. Immediately he was out of breath, but he didn't risk stopping, even for a second. He felt both nauseated and triumphant, as well as close to a heart attack. He slowed down, gasping a little, resting his hands on his knees. When he felt less dizzy, he started walking again, taking long strides. Did he really just do that? Nora would never believe it. He felt a wild laugh creep up his throat and choked it down. He really was out of control. What on earth had gotten into him?

The wind whistled at his back, pushing him towards home. By the time he got to the driveway, a pulse pounded in his head. The car was still there, Nora hadn't left yet, thank goodness. Maybe it was time to dig out his own suitcase. Maybe there was a little more left to him than either of them thought.

BINGO or Bust

By Lauranne Hemmingway

Bingo was a big deal with the ladies of my family, in the generation that came before. Aunts Mary, Barbara, and Dorothy often traveled to Fairview—some thirty miles away—for Sunday night bingo games. One Sunday night in autumn, they were off to Fairview, with Aunt Mary hinting that her left palm had been itchy all day—a sure sign of money headed her way. About bingo, she was the most exuberant of the trio. The others were happy to accompany her.

They were all engaged in conversation about family and friends – a wee bit of gossip and just a touch of criticism, when they noticed steam or smoke spewing from under the hood of the car. Someone suggested they get out before it exploded. Aunt Mary pulled over to the side of the road on the Dunvegan hill. She promptly opened the door and jumped out. Aunt Dorothy was in the middle seat. She knocked Aunt Barbara out of the passenger seat onto the ground in her haste to evacuate.

They were all out of the vehicle, when it began to slowly roll backwards, down the hill. Aunt Mary remembered a fortune teller's prophesy that summer that she would be driving a brand new vehicle. Two of the psychic's predictions had already come true. It looked like this one would come to pass as well.

The car seemed to be driven by some invisible force. Its path suddenly changed and it veered off the driving lane, and became suspended by the guard rail. The engine stalled and the steam no longer rolled out from under the hood.

Aunt Barbara was on the ground, looking a little stunned. Aunt Mary insisted she stand up, thereby demonstrating she had not broken any bones. When they were sure they were uninjured and the car no longer looked like it would explode, they began to plan their next steps.

As luck would have it, along came a neighbour, who stopped and checked the car. It needed a minor adjustment. The water hose clamp had come loose. He was able to repair it before going on his way. He assured the women that they could safely drive to Fairview or back home, whatever their choice.

"I think we should just call Tony. He will come and get us," was Aunt Dorothy's suggestion.

"I think we should go for coffee," was Aunt Mary's suggestion.

"We should get going to Fairview. We will be late for the bingo game if we don't go now," said Aunt Barbara.

They continued on to Fairview and were just a bit late for the first round of bingo.

Meanwhile, they were not winning and had calmed down, so they began to chat. Aunt Mary noticed that Aunt Barbara's face was dirty and her wig was on askew.

"Why didn't you tell me right away? It is little wonder that I am a mess! I was laying on the ground while the car tires came toward me and rolled over my hair."

"What were you thinking when that car was rolling toward you?", Aunt Mary had to know.

"I wasn't thinking. I was reading. Good Year, Good Year, Good Year!"

This is a story we all love to repeat in our family. It could have been tragic, but fortunately it was not. The fortune teller's prediction came to pass when Aunt Mary purchased a car, more to her liking. The passion for BINGO continued for several years—until she discovered lotteries.

Just My Luck

By Lyle Meeres

The Conservatives tax me
To give money to rich industrialists.
New Democrats want my money
To give it to the poor.
Just my luck—I'm middle class.

Some people are born into money.
They say I was born in the Depression.
I picked a profession which declares,
"We're not in it for the money."
Just my luck—we tell it like it is.

When I play cards for money
And the evening goes very well,
Someone's sure to say,
"Last hand—winner takes all."
Just my luck—I come in second.

[Cough, cough] I'm the quiet kind
You have to get to know [cough]
So not many do—except the happy
Gang that's lived in me forty days 'n nights.
Chest my luck—a friendly virus loves me.

In younger years, the pretty red-head
I chose to chase was a girl to 'no.'
She taught me to despise and disdain
All shades of red—but I hear it was
Just my luck—her husband feels the same.

I haven't won the Lotto yet, but then
I haven't been struck by lightning either.
So, given my luck, would I care to trade?
You bet, but the guy who was gonna trade—
Just my luck—got run over by a truck!

Some Assembly Required
By Lori M. Feldberg

*We sold our farm, bought a condo, and moved into half the house
space, no basement to store stuff, and a garage we have to sidle into
when the car is inside. Home sweet home! Of course, we made some
purchases to our new place, but it was not uneventful . . .*

Some assembly required. Not again! Those words sent a mixture of
panic and despair through me. Why is it you can't buy anything ready-
to-use anymore? Puzzles were never my forte and these purchases that
come in boxes that contain all manner of loose 'things', just isn't
something I want to spend time dealing with.

I gingerly tipped up the large cardboard box, knowing it was full of
parts and pieces. One 'Simplicity' model bathroom over-the-toilet
cabinet and stand, coming up–in 132 parts and pieces, *plus extras*!

Instructions, (*I call them warnings*), were written in English and
French (I think). The actual instructions were shown in diagram form on
twelve pages. I carefully laid out the fourteen wooden panels then the
seven Hardware Packs before Jim could get his hands on the little
packages. Those diagrams didn't offer much in the way of instruction.
Coupled with the fact that the three glue packs were dried up (just how
long did this 'last' box sit on the shelf?), and the inevitable mystery
arrows, sometimes pointing the wrong way, it took a *mere* six hours to
assemble with screws and wooden dowels, then place over our toilet.

It didn't help that our toilet is backed into a space between the wall
and the shower, leading me to believe the toilet was installed first. We
couldn't put the stand together beforehand—had to do it around the toilet,
which makes me ask, *'How many toilets do you find out in the middle of
the floor with access all around'*? There was no room to get a
screwdriver in there, so I had to use a jack knife while lying on the
concrete floor with my face pressed into the base of the toilet. Yuk!
Couldn't they invent a cabinet stand more suited to the toilet being placed
against the wall (like *all* toilets are)?

Anyway, it was off to bed at 10:30 p.m., after six hours of sweat and toil, substitute pieces, and choice words. At least we were getting speedier at this business.

Not so quick was the first project. That one took two days to assemble. Now, there was the purchase that came as a total surprise.

We bought a lovely ceramic (or some sort of ceramic/plastic-coated pressboard) electric fireplace from Canadian Tire. Part of our decision to take one based on the attractive all-put-together-and-working display, was that it was lighter than some, and of a size that we could handle ourselves.

Imagine our dismay, after we lugged the box into the house and prepared to carefully extract our new purchase, when we discovered that it wasn't ready to plug in. No indeedy—it wasn't even remotely ready to use, and there was no '*Some Assembly Required*' warning on the box! Out spilled 218 pieces, plus spare parts.

Actually, I didn't know how many pieces and parts there were to start with. I was doing other things, and not aware of the major trouble looming ahead of me. I didn't threaten my husband with bodily harm—should he decide to tackle this project before I could help him—which I would have (threatened him, that is) had I known the complexity of it and the total lack of disregard he paid for instructions or all those little packages of hardware!

By the time I turned to the chaos on my living room floor (after listening to him vent his opinion of the ridiculous trend to 'do-it-yourself'), he had *pooled* all the packages of hardware, unintentionally, of course, and put some panels together incorrectly. I must admit, that even had he read the complex but still confusing instructions in any of the four languages shown, he probably wouldn't have figured it out anyway.

Now he wondered why things weren't matching up properly. It didn't help that someone in the packaging department had incorrectly, or maybe deliberately (a little worker revenge or something) stuck some of the indicator arrows facing the wrong way. We had to take some panels apart and try again.

We tried for two days to assemble that thing. There were some words said. There were a lot of words unsaid, too.

Jim was all for forgetting about putting the little halogen lights in. We just couldn't seem to find the way to install them, per instruction. That was one of the things that we *(he)* liked about the fireplace, and his frustration was showing when he said, not exactly mild of manner, "Forget them!"

Finally, I realized that those nasty packing men (no women would have been this mean, I'm sure) had assembled the lights incorrectly just for the sake of keeping the parts together. I must have looked at those diagrams and the assembled lights for a couple of hours before I figured that out. Then in no time I had them apart, reassembled and installed.

Did I mention that it took two days to put that #$*& thing together! I swore we wouldn't do another *Some Assembly Required* project again. Not two weeks later, we bought the bathroom cabinet I already told you about. But, this time, I insisted that the box remain sealed until I was ready to help keep those little packages of hardware separate and designated to each portion of the job!

Cars with Character

By Lyle Meeres

My wife Pat and I learned that cars can have quirks that give them personality. When our son was born, we bought a big, ancient Hudson that had two of everything under the hood. This meant it was fast: double your pleasure... double your expenses. When it broke down we had to replace two of whatever it was. And the car was missing one vital component: a speedometer that worked.

When we had to go to Calgary, we would follow a car we thought was going about the right speed. Our judgement was not always good. We remember one particular trip our parents never heard about. We followed a car that seemed to be going the right speed. However, when we got to Calgary, we realized we must have been following a stray from NASCAR. The time we set is still a family record.

Another problem I had with the car came one day when I drove to work, to the elementary school. When I pulled in to the curb, a policeman I knew from my work with school patrols came up to my car window. He asked the usual question: "Do you know how fast you were going?" I gave him the truthful answer: "No." He told me to slow down in the school zone and let me off with a warning. It would not look good if the teacher in charge of the school's safety patrols got a speeding ticket.

My Dad picked out our second car which was a small but newer little foreign job. Slower, but newer. During the summer, it was great, but when winter came, its little quirk was nasty. We could have heat, or we could see out by using the defroster. We could not have heat AND defrost. Around the city that wasn't too bad, but we had to drive to Edmonton for Christmas because it was Pat's parents' turn to have us share the season, and they would not want to miss seeing our two adorable little kids.

Of course it turned bitterly cold the day we hit the highway. We bundled the kids up as well as we could, then wrapped them in blankets in the back seat. Nonetheless, we all froze. Eventually we reached

Edmonton city limits. With the dense Christmas traffic I had to see, so I opened my side window and peered out. Then we froze everything that had previously had blood circulating, plus we got gassed by all the exhausts.

Later, we bought a little old beater that had a heater and all. It was our 'holy' car. Its little quirk was that the floorboard behind the gas pedal had rusted through. In fact it had just plain vanished. It's quite a feeling to drive along and see the road zipping along under your feet when you aren't even pedaling. The garage where I had the car serviced took pity on us and fastened a metal plate from a defunct refrigerator over the hole in the floor. No more 'holy' car. Much better!

Our fourth car was a massive Meteor that had a heater that actually worked. It also had a big motor. The first time I took it out on the highway, on another trip to Edmonton, I got a speeding ticket.

We eventually got a sporty Comet. By then our son Michael could drive, and he terrorized his mother by zipping around corners on the highway driving west to join me camping.

Time passed and we bought a Pontiac that had as its quirk a huge magnet that attracted other vehicles to it. One day we were sitting in our house and the doorbell rang. A red-faced young woman who was learning to drive apologized that she had smacked into our car which was parked out front. We had that damage repaired. However, one evening I was driving to a curling game when a car zinged through a red light and creamed me. Concussion city—there were no seat belts then.

Since that time our cars have been more sedate, solid citizens. And that's not all bad.

The weakness of modern cars is the lack of character. There's no drama... unless you count recalls... or unless you count manufacturers who cheat on emission statistics. These add up to thousands of cars. There is nothing individual about all those cars getting new air bags— someday—and all those car owners getting cheques to make up for poor resale value. I miss the individuality of the old cars.

Beaver Dams and Trout Streams

by John Burnham

On the white sandy beach of a South Sea island, Prime Minister Alphonse Arsenault reclined in a lounge chair. Music from a satellite feed wafted softly from the villa. Bountiful bosoms bounced to the beat. A gentle breeze rustled the palm leaves. As a servant boy completed the latest refill of his glass, it happened—the music went dead. The bosoms stopped bouncing. Angrily, the PM yelled toward the villa, "Turn the damn music back on."

"Working on it," came back faintly.

Alphonse relaxed and regarded the clear, azure sky. The warmth surrounded him in a mellow embrace. It was damn nice of Northern Omega Oil to loan him their little private piece of paradise for a well-earned holiday. If he played his cards right, he'd have a beautiful, unspoiled place like this for his retirement. The girls milled about, giggling uncertainly. The heat, inactivity, and alcohol took their toll. Arsenault drifted off.

A few minutes later, Chris McDonald—the head of his legal staff—gently shook his shoulder. Reluctant to leave the cozy stupor, Arsenault growled, "What the hell is it?"

"Sorry to wake you Chief, but we have a situation."

"Can't th' damn thing wait?"

"I think we need to give this an answer as soon as communications are restored."

Arsenault became alert. "Restored?"

"Yes," McDonald replied. "The music went off because the feed from the satellite died. All the other communication channels quit at the same time. The techies are working on it. Anyway, just before everything went quiet, I received a communiqué from the legal leeches. It seems the L'itsuk band has retained legal counsel. They are suing."

The PM reached for his glass and took a deliberate drink. "I told ya; I don't give a rat's ass about a few beaver dams and trout streams."

McDonald swallowed. "This action isn't restricted to the damage being done in their local area, sir. They have allied with other bands to have some large-scale research done. The action alleges damage to the entire watershed system and the livelihood of hundreds of people."

Alphonse turned to look directly at McDonald. "You think the damage assessment is good?"

"Yes, sir. If we don't force Northern Omega to comply with the toxic waste disposal regulations, that entire area will become a wasteland."

"And what will happen if we clamp down on Northern Omega?"

"They've already advised that the project would become financially untenable."

The PM sniffed. "So, bright boy, what do you think we should tell the legal people?"

"Well, sir, ah...it's complicated...and..."

Arsenault's countenance darkened. "Complicated, my ass. We mess with Northern Omega, they pull out, the Yanks have to buy their oil somewhere else, and we wind up holdin' the bag. You tell the legal weasels to put the whole watershed thing in the same bag as beaver dams and trout streams. We ain't stoppin' progress and that's it!"

McDonald opened his mouth to speak, but the PM waved him off. He'd heard the approaching security officer shout something about an emergency. "Emergency?" Alphonse queried as the man approached.

"Communications sir. We've lost all contact with the rest of the world. All the satellite feeds are dead!"

Alphonse groped at his pocket. "Where's my cell?"

The Security Officer shook his head. "It won't do you any good, sir. The communications tech has tried all the cellular satellites. None of them are responding."

Arsenault's brow wrinkled. "All entertainment and communication satellites down at the same time?"

The Security Officer shrugged. "Yes, sir. As far as we can tell, that is the situation."

Arsenault stood. "There's gotta be a hunnerd or more of them things. They all got their own power. How could they all go kaput at the same time?"

The Security Officer waved a hand as if to dismiss the imponderables of the question. "I have no answer for that sir. However, the unknowns of this situation make it imperative that we get you home ASAP."

The engines of the private jet were whining as Arsenault, still clad in shorts and a flowered shirt, strode across the tarmac. A young woman, dressed in the Northern Omega Oil uniform, greeted him as he entered the aircraft. "Welcome, Mr. Prime Minister. Please have a seat. We should be off in a few minutes. May I get you a beverage?"

"Uh, I wanna talk to the pilot—see if he knows what's goin' on."

The woman stepped aside and gestured toward the front. "Certainly, sir."

Stepping into the cockpit, Alphonse was surprised to see the co-pilot's seat unoccupied. The pilot turned questioningly as he slid one earphone back on his head. "Uh, I thought there was supposed to be two 'o you guys," the PM said.

"My co-pilot is in the villa. He's trying Northern Omega's emergency communications access."

"Yeah? What might he be able to do that my guys couldn't?"
The pilot squirmed.

Arsenault glared. "Look son, I'm the Prime Minister of your country."

"Uh, sir, Northern Omega does have access to the Trans-Pacific cable and to the U.S. Navy's permanent sonar arrays. We're not supposed to use them unless it's a matter of life and death."

So, Northern Omega has tricks up their sleeve that they haven't told my people about, eh, Arsenault thought with aggravation. His pique abated as the last of the pilot's words sank in. "Life and death?" he blurted.

The pilot did a deep breathing exercise as he looked about the cockpit in confusion. "Sir, I'm afraid that I can't make contact with any of the Global Positioning Satellites. Moreover, we can't make contact with anybody to find out about en route weather."

"So?"

"I need GPS to find Hawaii. We can't take off without knowing the weather conditions."

With irritation, the PM replied, "I thought this thing flew above the weather."

His voice tinged with impatience, the pilot answered, "Our optimum cruising altitude does put us above most of the weather, but tropical storms can exceed our maximum altitude."

"So, fly through it!"

"Sir, that extent of vertical development in a storm would indicate severe turbulence—very possibly beyond the structural limitations of this aircraft."

"Then, hell, you just fly around it."

The pilot began to look like he was talking to a retarded child. "Sir, this aircraft does not leave the ground without a weather briefing."

The PM's face grew red. His fists clenched. As he started to speak, the co-pilot appeared in the door. The pilot's features relaxed as he turned away from the confrontation. "How does it look?"

The co-pilot shook his head. "No joy. The cable is flooded with traffic; it's impossible to get a connection. We get no response on any radio frequency, so we can't establish contact with a ship or offshore rig that would get us patched into the Navy's sonar array."

Threateningly, Alphonse blurted, "I'll tell you two what you're gonna do. You're gonna get this damn thing into the air and fly it to Hawaii. If we run into any weather, you can figure out what to do then!"

The pilot looked at the co-pilot, reached for the throttles, and pulled them back into the shutdown position.

Arsenault's eyes widened as the whine of the engines died. "What the hell?" he shouted.

The pilot flipped a few switches and began to unfasten his seat belt. "Without GPS, my chances of finding Hawaii are not much better than nil."

"What kinda pilot are you? Don't you have a compass or sumpthin'?"

The pilot lifted himself out of the seat. Wearily, he looked at his antagonist. "There's a thousand miles of open ocean between here and

Hawaii. You do the math. An error of a degree or two would mean we'd never see it."

The PM stomped his foot. He raised his fist. Blood vessels stood out on his forehead. "You impudent little cuss! When I get done, you won't be pilotin' a shopping cart."

"At least, I'll be alive," the pilot replied as he pushed past Alphonse's bulk.

That night, there was an unusual glow on the northern horizon. Speculation ran rampant that somebody had pushed the nuclear button.

The co-pilot and the stewardess—certain that the pilot's defiance of Arsenault had saved their lives—didn't hesitate to relate details of the encounter to the rest of the staff. Soon, the appellation, "Alphonse 'The Arrogant' Arsenault" given to the PM by the media, was heard during conversation.

For the remainder of that day and the following two days, anxiety grew. People speculated about apocalypse, tsunami, and how long the food and water would last. The Arrogant one fumed and stomped about. Whether they verbalized it or not, the entire staff experienced moments of comic relief watching Arsenault in a situation he couldn't control by bluster and intimidation.

During the third night, the glow disappeared. Electronic devices came back on line. Information began pouring in. Unfortunately, most of it regarded rescue and relief efforts, but it was clear that the event was unprecedented. Communications, including GPS, had been knocked out worldwide. An undetermined number of airliners had lost their way, run out of fuel or collided with other craft. Every form of transportation that employed electronic control or monitoring had been similarly affected. Railroad tracks were strewn with train wrecks. Roads and streets were scenes of vehicular carnage. Nobody knew exactly why.

Arsenault put everybody except the pilot and co-pilot to the task of combing the news feeds for anything that reported on what had actually happened. The bits and pieces delivered to him conjured a most disturbing picture: The event itself was thermonuclear, but of a nature that defied description. The location was unfortunate—the Arctic boundary of his own country. Not only had the most disruptive occurrence in history happened on his watch, it had happened on his turf and, dammit, while he was away! He jumped to his feet and shouted, "What the hell are those flyboys doin'? Why ain't we in the air?" An aide meekly handed him a cell phone.

"This is your co-pilot, sir," was the calm reply from the instrument.

"Whaddya jerk-offs doin'? Why ain't we in the air?"

"I was just about to inform you sir, that we have obtained Air Traffic Control clearance. Our assigned departure time is…er…one hour and fifty-two minutes from now."

Alphonse spun on his heel and stomped. "Two hours? No damn way! I'm comin' right out and takeoff will be immediate!"

In a tone that might as well be asking "Double-double with that?" the co-pilot replied, "Sir, the system is jammed by rescue and disaster-control efforts. We were told we'd have to wait at least five days for clearance until we pointed out that we were carrying the head of state for the country in which the event occurred. In…ah…one hundred and ten minutes, we will be rolling down the runway. If this aircraft takes to the air any sooner than that, we will not be at the controls."

Arsenault threw the cell phone into a nearby fishbowl.

During the flight from the island to Hawaii and then back home, Arsenault and his aides continued to sift through incoming information. From conflicting reports and fragmented data, a picture gradually emerged. There was a pit on the northern border of his country, approximately round, about two hundred kilometres in diameter, and more than a kilometre deep. Strangely, speculation had died off about who had caused it or why.

Alphonse sat back and rubbed his eyes. The opposition and their toady press were going to have a field day with this. They'd dubbed him Alphonse "The Arrogant" Arsenault, claiming he ran the country like a private banana republic. His absence during this event would augment their characterization of him as a self-indulgent petty despot. No matter, the people who counted—the ones holding the purse strings—

liked the way he did things. He had to ensure that this event, whatever it was, didn't affect their interests. In order to do that, he needed information he did not have. Fortunately, as near as he could ascertain from the available data, nobody else did either.

As the aircraft circled for landing, The Arrogant One stared through the window in disbelief. The city, his city, the capital of his country, was a mess: Traffic was stalled on several major arteries due to massive accident scenes. Smoke rose from burning buildings here and there. In the vicinity of the airport, he could count at least three sites where aircraft had crashed into populated areas.

Arsenault was a bundle of fury as he bounded out of the airplane and into the waiting limo. Upon entering the vehicle, he burst into a torrent of questions. "Why the hell are those buildings afire? Where is the fire department? Why hasn't that mess been cleared from the 101?"

When The Arrogant One finally ran down, he noticed that the aide he was yelling at wasn't wearing a tie, had a couple of day's growth of beard, and dark circles under his eyes. The man ran a hand through uncombed hair and answered wearily, "It's a matter of priority, sir. When the electronics went dead, all manner of control systems failed and fires broke out all over the place. The fire department is overwhelmed; we have to allocate equipment in an order that will minimize loss of life. Unfortunately, that means some fires will be left to burn themselves out. The freeways are a similar problem. Every single one was shut down by accidents. We're clearing by priority, but they won't all be running until sometime next week."

Arsenault was red in the face. "What's wrong with you guys? Why didn't you weenies call out the National Guard?"

The aide massaged the back of his own neck as he stretched his head wearily. "Sir, the National Guard has been mobilized. Every city in the country has the same problem, so they are spread very thin. It is only due to their help that we are able to keep our clean-up efforts going around the clock." The man dropped his head and looked down at his lap. "Unfortunately, that may not continue for long."

Alphonse's gaze snapped from the scene outside to the man across from him. "Whazzat supposed to mean?"

"Fuel sir. Delivery has been disrupted and we only have a few days' supply left."

Prime Minister Alphonse Arsenault glared across his massive desk at the closed door. Rundle wasn't due for another ten minutes. Still, he willed his Chief of Intelligence to walk through that door. The most important event in hundreds of years—perhaps in all of human history —had happened on his watch and, he still didn't know what it was. He ground his teeth in frustration and impatiently drummed his fingers on the desk. He needed distraction. He flipped open a folder that had been placed on the middle of his desk. A condescending smirk formed on his lips as he read.

The document was a brief on the L'itsuk action to sue his government. Sure enough, they were claiming environmental disaster had resulted from the government's failure to enforce policy. They were right, of course. Northern Omega Oil was playing fast and loose with their handling of waste products, but the country needed the oil, and his party needed the campaign contributions. What difference did the ruination of a few beaver dams and trout streams make anyway? The brief went on to delineate the rage and impotence felt by the affected people. A secondary action requested compensation for mental and emotional distress. *So what?,* thought The Arrogant One as he flipped the folder closed. The office door opened. A tall, greying man strode through. Gary Rundle didn't look as well-groomed as usual, the PM noted. Maybe he'd been up all night. Good. Maybe he had something.

"Good morning Chief," Rundle said as he sank wearily into a chair.

"Whaddya got?"

Rundle pulled papers from his attaché case. "We now know that the affected area was approximately cylindrical in shape and about two hundred kilometres in diameter."

"Any idea how high?"

"No."

"Anybody try to fly over it?"

"The Yanks sent a blackbird up. It hasn't been heard from since."

"The bastards wouldn't tell us if it did find the top."

"I don't think it did. The laser equipment still worked, so we were able to track it. Like everything else that tried an overfly, it disappeared. In fact, there may be some wreckage where the bottom of the cylinder was."

"Is it still too hot to get in there?"

"Yes, the radiation levels look like Chernobyl."

"How about a team wearing those protective suits?"

Rundle took a deep breath as he lifted his gaze above the PM's face. "I don't think that's a good idea either."

Arsenault rested his elbow on the desk and put his chin against the palm of his hand. This sounded like more bad news. His fingers massaged his temple. "Wanna tell me why not?"

Rundle extracted a paper and referred to it briefly. His eyes regained contact with the PM's. "The Israelis sent in a team wearing hot suits on the second day. Now, they all show signs of radiation poisoning."

The Arrogant One's head came off his hand. His brow furrowed. "Ain't that too fast? Don't radiation poisoning take months to show up?"

"It depends on the intensity of the exposure, but yes, this is very rapid. The most troubling aspect is that it occurred through the protection of the hot suits."

"Was the suits top-drawer?"

"The Israelis have the best. That's where we buy ours. Their failure to protect the wearers suggests we are dealing with an unknown type of radiation—a particle that the suits can't stop."

"How about the other people?"

Rundle extracted another report and studied it. He didn't raise his head as he read. "All of our people that were within a kilometre are showing signs of radiation poisoning. Friendly nations, the Brits, French, Germans, Yanks, and so on, report the same. People like the Chinese, Iranians, and North Koreans are asking for information about rapid-onset radiation poisoning. So, it's a safe bet their teams suffered the same fate."

Arsenault's face grew red. "I knew the rug-heads had people in there, but I can't believe we let a piss-ant little outfit like North Korea get a team in."

Rundle leaned back and regarded his boss patiently. "On Day Two, that cylinder was brighter than the sun. It reached into the stratosphere. There wasn't any place in the Northern Hemisphere where you couldn't see either it or the light from it. Every government on the planet made investigating it their top priority. I can tell you which teams made it in before the cylinder disappeared," Rundle concluded as he began to flip through his pile of paper.

The PM waived a hand dismissively. "Nah, spare me the details. Has anybody tried to fly over the area since the thing left?"

"Yes, the Russians had a Bear orbiting the site. It tried an overfly at thirty-three thousand feet."

"And?"

"It got about ten kilometres inside the edge of where the cylinder had been. Apparently, ashes were all that hit the bottom of the pit."

"My god! A column of radiation that fried an airplane at thirty-three thousand feet! What could make something like that?"

Rundle took another deep breath. "Nothing on this planet."

Alarm began to show on The Arrogant One's face. "What's that supposed to mean?"

"That thing was a contained thermonuclear reaction. The energy output was phenomenal. The ability to produce, much less contain, something of that magnitude is quite beyond the capacity of anybody on this earth."

"Any guesses as to what it was all about?"

"I'd think a mining operation of some sort."

"Why do you say that?"

"We sent a drone over the site a few hours ago. It sent back good information before it got fried. The thing left a hole more than twenty kilometres deep. The sides are vertical. A chunk of the earth's crust two hundred kilometres in diameter and twenty plus kilometres thick is missing. That column of radioactive dust is the only sign of the missing material. Typically, when we reduce rock to dust, we're mining something."

The PM waived his hand to indicate he didn't want to hear any more about mining. "That bunch of radioactive dust, which direction is it goin'?"

"The prevailing winds will take it northeast, over the pole."

The Arrogant One smirked. "Fried Ivan eh?"

"Yes, Russia will be the first to experience fallout."

"You said the radioactive stuff is worse than anything we—I mean every country—has messed with?"

"Yes, it's like a bomb that's dirtier than anything we thought possible."

"Worse than—whaddya call it—a...a...neutron bomb?"

"Precisely so. There are subatomic particles pouring out of that dust we don't know anything about. The only thing we do know is that signs of radiation poisoning appear almost immediately after exposure."

Unconsciously, the PM rubbed his hands together in satisfaction. "So, Ivan's in for it."

Discomfort registered on Rundle's face. He shifted in his chair. "Yes, but we won't be far behind."

Hands parted and slammed flat on the desk as Arsenault came out of his chair shouting, "Whaddya mean?"

The Arrogant One was half standing, his face becoming flushed. Rundle looked at him with the calmness reserved for those who have nothing left to lose. "Within thirty days, the jet stream will have carried that cloud around the world. There is enough contaminated material floating around up there to produce a mass extinction. It will rival anything that has happened before."

Arsenault fell back into his chair with wide, frightened eyes. As he alternately looked at the ceiling, the walls, and out the window, his expression became less frightened and more cunning. After several minutes, he spoke. "Ok, here's what I want you to do..."

Rundle interrupted by standing. Across a slightly trembling lower lip, he said, "With all due respect, I suggest you tell it to my replacement.

What I am going to do is go home and spend whatever time I have left with my family."

Colour rose again in The Arrogant One's face. "You can't do that. This is a national emergency; we're under attack." Blood vessels began to pop out in his forehead as he watched a sardonic smile form on his subordinate's face.

"Attack is the wrong word. We've been exploited," Rundle said simply and turned toward the door without picking up his attaché case or papers.

A stream of vituperation erupted from Alphonse as Rundle walked. Wearily, he paused and turned around. "I almost forgot," he said quietly and waited for the tirade to cease.

Arsenault ended with, "Well, give!"

"I said the hole was approximately twenty kilometres deep because the actual bottom is obscured by the products of seismic activity."

"Seismic which, what?"

"Like volcanoes. The crust of the earth at the bottom of that hole has been weakened and fractured. There is a high probability that the whole thing will become volcanic."

The PM began to look drained. "That sounds bad."

"It is worse than bad. An eruption would fill the atmosphere with enough volcanic dust to block out the sun."

Fear regained dominance of Arsenalt's features. "Who or what could have done such a terrible thing to us?"

Rundle shook his head slowly while he looked at the PM. He pointed to the folder on the desk. "Remember why you said we weren't going to do anything about that?"

The Arrogant One looked at the folder outlining the L'itsuk band's suit. "I...ah...said we couldn't let a few beaver dams and trout streams stand in the way of progress."

Rundle gave a thin, condescending, smile. "Whoever did this probably regarded our great cities and magnificent agricultural systems as 'beaver dams and trout streams' — nothing that should impede their idea of progress."

"It's unconscionable, uncivilized..."

Rundle began to look amused. "On the contrary, I think it's quite typical of civilized people."

"This ain't the time for riddles."

"My apologies. It just struck me that whoever produced this phenomenon is treating us exactly as our ancestors treated the indigenous people of this continent. In fact, it's typical of the way civilized people have always treated less technically advanced cultures."

When his boss didn't reply, Rundle turned and started toward the door. Before stepping through it, he turned around and said, "Perhaps what happened to us is poetic justice. Goodbye."

Prime Minister Alphonse (The Arrogant) Arsenault didn't move for many minutes after Rundle's departure. Although crude, he wasn't stupid. He now understood that there wasn't going to be any retirement on an island paradise. An uncaring superior power had destroyed his cherished dreams. He looked down at the folder. The paragraph delineating the anger and helplessness felt by the people he was destroying appeared in his mind. Suddenly, he felt cold inside. The rage and impotence felt by the L'itsuk band did not feel good in his own chest.

"Thank-You"
By Robert Swann

When the entire world comes down
And everything seems to fall
Be thankful for solace that's ever present
Be of good cheer,
for I have overcome the world.
Jesus has comfort and confidence.
The battle is already won.
John 16:33

The Prosecutor
By Michelle T. Lambert

S-S-
sneaky
prodding
and
provoking
conspiring
unscrupulous
positioned to
pounce.
Orange-
Speckled
forked-
tongued
relentlessly
attacking
acutely
ready
to strike.
Incessantly
Torturing
Puncturing
and subduing
its victim.
Still turning
and twisting
suddenly
tightening
constricting
and
choking
now
puncturing
with
one last
victorious
venomous
bite.

Murderer

By Cole Farwell

Today I murdered a dream, mine, in cold blood.
Not in the fires of passion!
Not in the darkness of defeat...
But in the idle calculations of practicality.
I now feel a gaping emptiness in my chest.

In this hollowed state, I have achieved some clairvoyance.
I see my dream now, dropped and shattered.
For I was too afraid to run with it.
On the brink of a leap of faith, I backed down, in fear of failure.
And now it's too late... The time passed; my dream now cold in its grave.

I'm left now with only questions and regret.
Is this taking a step into adulthood?
Or a coward's way out?

Four Directions
By Robert Swann

VERY BIG POSITIVE
Watch where you're going
Looking back, you can't move ahead
Add more, the daily ups and downs
Outside is showy, inside is important
Where are you? X with a twist hits the spot
On the mark and centralized

Every Mother

By Michelle T. Lambert

For days I carry an unknown weight:
an oppressive moroseness and heaviness
penetrates my soul and seeks to burrow
into every nook and cranny of my being.

This oppression grips my spirit
just like bramble bushes
cling to my clothes.

Then I begin to see the face of a woman
who weeps and mourns.
She is a Sorrowful Mother.
She is the Mother Sorrowful.

She grieves for all women, who past and present
throughout eternity,
are misunderstood, lonely, hated, used and defiled,
tolerated if unseen and unheard.

Her *chador* hides her and her identity, like a shroud.
Amidst the daily struggles of her life,
and the conflicting thoughts and questions that pierce her soul,
an unknown sadness and a mysterious longing invade her being.

Suddenly her child stirs beside her. It whimpers and cries.
She reaches down and picks it up, cradling it to her breast.
The child, now at peace, is quiet
and the mother, relieved, feels
infinite love and maternal tenderness.

The night unfolds and a new light dawns.

_____

Chador: A long loose cloak, usually black, worn over garments by
some Muslim women, consisting of a long semicircular piece of cloth
draped over the hair and shoulders to cover the body from head to foot,
as well as most of the face.

The Unknowing
By Alison Whittmire

There is a quest for a Knowing
upon which we all embark.
It is a quest for insight,
for the quiet confidence
that comes from finding The Truth
and holding it in the palm of your hand.

We study scriptures and summersault across foreign lands
until the day when we find it and hold onto it, and it is *ours*!
As our fingers grasp the Knowing, the sly curl on our lips
cannot help but reveal the profound satisfaction
that accompanies the completion of a successful journey.
Oh, how delicious is this moment of victory!

Most times, we store our Knowing upon a shelf,
in plain view and accessible, yet just far enough out of reach
to convey that this is *ours*, that *we* earned it!
Yet, every once in a while, when we ache for it to be a part of us again,
we pluck it from the shelf and lovingly caress it amongst our fingers,
waiting for its wisdom to seep warmly inside.

Then there are moments when we yearn to share our potent treasure:
sometimes by tenderly transferring it to the trembling,
outstretched hand of a curious seeker;
Other times, by hurling it recklessly as a violent spear
intended to pierce and deflate our target's intellectual refuge,
as our chests puff out boastfully with undeserved pride.

Oh, how I wish I had realized, that we would all understand,
that each and every spear we'd throw would come back
to pierce our own sides!
For the moment of Knowing is followed by an unravelling
where all that we thought was certain and forever withers away
and our real journey can begin.

For the Truth is not ours to hold.
The Truth is alive! It breathes and grows!
And surely life cannot be sustained on shelf or in pocket.
These are the spaces that shells of lives gone by occupy.
They solidify and remain stagnant while all that is vibrant and animate
slips through our fingers like desert sand.

Rather, on rare and fortunate occasion,
when stillness sneaks upon us and coaxes us to let go of all that we
Know,
we are gifted with a single grain,
a glowing ember that shines white hot for but a second
before being snuffed out by ego's beckoning
that the dirt on our hands must be washed away.

Yet, one by one, moment by moment, we begin to trust the grains of
sand.
With clarity, for the first time, we understand that we do not stand on
dirt,
but rather on the infinite history of our ancestors and all that they are
and all that we will one day be. And with this realization, a mighty
crescendo
exhales from deep within, as our hearts begin to pulse in
synchronization
with the rhythm of all that is, and all that can never be known.

Medicine Wheel

By Robert Swann

The circle cycles, one point on one point, on and on
The return, back to the beginning, start again
Everything seems to go in circles
Reasons, Seasons REPEAT
Over again, recycled
Thankfully

Moonlight Whispers

By Alison Whittmire

Sometimes,
When I lie alone
in the murky, shadowy stillness
of the midnight hour,
that trickster Doubt,
slyly, cunningly,
slinks under the door.

Convincing me,
with impeccable logic,
if even for a moment,
that hope is pointless,
foolish, uneducated,
naive.
I almost acquiesce.

But then, on absolute perfect cue,
a single sliver of silver Moonlight
trickles through the window
and kisses my weary palm.
I am bathed, enveloped,
in both passion and compassion
for myself, my future.

Moonlight reminds me,
with equal parts kindness and resolve
that Hope is neither logic nor naiveté.
Hope is power. Hope is intuition.
It is the visceral knowing
that the condition of my body need *not*
dictate whether or not I am healed.

All I have is hope.
And that is a lot.

Chevron
By Robert Swann

Representing mountains and valleys
I love the lakes and rivers, the hills too
I don't like taking water to the top
Rough and tough, no easy ride
Onward, upward, downer, reality
Bring it on, over and again

To Oblivion

By Cole Farwell

Minute to Minute,
Hour to Hour,
Day to Day,
Our lives pass by...
Winds ever blowing.
Waters endlessly flowing.
Occasionally we find ourselves in the midst of significance,
Days that forever burn themselves into our minds.
Often in the very moment it seems all too surreal,
As we navigate a storm of emotion.
Bombarded on all sides by the voices of near strangers,
On how these moments fit into the big picture,
As if they could know.
These moments are destined by one means or another.
Some arrive precisely, every detail planned out. Others come to us
through means of chance and coincidence; they arrive at random.
Seemingly created from nothing.
Order to Chaos,
Day to Night,
Life to Death,
To each, a beautiful eternity is given, only to be delicately swept away in
a river of time.

Stillness

By Alison Whittmire

I sit in stillness
Silently
And wonder
Where am I going?
Thoughts racing fervently.
What can I do
To become
The person I should be?

I sit in stillness
Silently
And wonder
What about this moment?
Thoughts slowing down
Beginning
To understand
The person that I am.

I sit in stillness
Silently
And realize
That it is not about wondering.
Thoughts are gone.
With clarity I now
Understand
That it is in the silence that I become.

I Do Declare
By Robert Swann

A sense of belonging
Overcoming opponents
Love, God, Peace
Defined in weakness
Depression is terrible
Innocence gone
At the name of Jesus Christ
Question Suicide
Why so despaired
Why so convincing
Value of life's endeavor
Personal, Social, Effect
Friend, Counsel, Nature
Almighty, Respect, Precious
Deliverance in forgiveness
Strategy of prayer
Repent and rebuke the Enemy

I Wish For You Nothing.

By Alison Whittmire

So many of us belong to families, workplaces, peer groups and societies that equate success with productivity. We are told in both overt and subtle ways that we are doing *nothing* when we wait. Stillness is considered unproductive. Wasted time. And, in the midst of being inundated with this life philosophy, we often respond by internalizing it and glorifying busyness. "Just keep going" is the mantra we repeat as we over-schedule ourselves and our children, brag about how much overtime we work, sign up for evening classes, and volunteer. Ah, yes, they myth of achieving success through busyness! This is the narrative we are bombarded with, cling to, and celebrate over and over and over. With white knuckles, we fiercely and falsely hold onto the belief that the more we do, the more we are thriving in the game of life! We are convinced that the busier we are, the more we accomplish, and that is through sheer tenacity to keep up with incredible rates of activity that our wildest dreams can be achieved! We keep pressing forward with no finish line in sight, infinitely surrounded by the millions upon millions who run this race in lock step with us.

We live in a society where it takes a conscious effort and it is an uphill battle just to set boundaries that enable us to carve out a space for stillness and silence. Yet, it is in our stillest and quietest moments that ideas are formed, insights are shared, bodies are repaired, and our purpose and direction become illuminated. We often squash opportunities for sharing, bonding, insight and healing because we have an incessant need to fill up a room with talking, movement, busyness, something, *anything*! And, while this approach to life may work well for many of us for quite some time, and it may even contribute to many of our personal and professional accomplishments, it also brings with it the danger of making us bone weary and not well connected to who and *why* we are. For, the notion of achieving success through busyness is *indeed* a myth and we cannot and will not be fooled by this myth forever. Our bodies and our minds and our relationships are not able to keep up with a light speed pace, and, inevitably, sooner or later, something is bound to break. It is at this fracturing point, and through this gift of brokenness, that we are finally able to realize that life's successes are not accomplished only through our actions. They are achieved through our successful interactions between work and stillness. It is a dance. A perfect balance.

With this in mind, I sincerely, from the bottom of my heart, wish for you nothing. Each and every single day I wish for you moments of stillness. I hope that you will take every opportunity to fully engage in the pauses of life's dance. I wish for you to embrace and cherish and celebrate the still moments of supposed nothingness that connect our steps and transform them from a whirlwind of meaningless, choreographed, jittery movements, into a work of art and a powerful and beautiful story. I participated in a yoga class where the instructor concluded with the following statement: "Remember that success is not determined by what you do, but by who you become." These words continue to echo in my mind They are a powerful reminder that success does not live at some illusive finish line any more than pots of gold at the end of rainbows. No, success lives in us when make the brave decision to do less but become more, to exit the race and enter the dance.

ABOUT THE AUTHORS

John A. Burnham grew up in Denver, Colorado. He served in the U.S. Navy and has enjoyed employment in manufacturing, aviation, and the oilpatch. Now, a full time writer, he has one novel, two plays, numerous articles and newspaper columns to his writing credits. He currently lives in Red Deer, Alberta, Canada.

Cole Farwell is an aspiring young writer from Red Deer Alberta; he's working on the revision of his of first novel. He has a passion for travel, and the adventures that come with it. Cole enjoys spending his time rock climbing, hiking, and hanging out with friends & family. Of course, he also loves to write.

Lori Feldberg of Wetaskiwin, is a prolific writer with traditional and self-published books to her credit, along with works in news and literary magazines, and in anthologies like 'Chicken Soup for the Soul'. She writes in a wide variety of genres with humour being a key part of many.

Jenna Hanger currently works at a newspaper in Ad Sales, putting her Communication Arts diploma to use. She pursues her passion for writing in her spare time. After leaving her home in Brownfield, AB Jenna now lives with her husband in Red Deer, AB and is expecting their first child.

Lauranne Hemmingway is a writer since her retirement from a career in social work. She joined Writers' Ink and enjoys the feedback and educational opportunities offered by the group. Her continued fascination with people is evident in her short stories. A native Albertan, she now calls Innisfail her home.

Judy Jackson was born and raised on a farm near Elnora, Alberta. Presently residing in Red Deer, Alberta.

Michelle T. Lambert hails from a French-Canadian community in BC. She later moved to Edmonton, AB and became a teacher. A woman's writing group encouraged her love of words. She works as a teacher/tutor, and continues to hone her skills as a writer of poetry and short stories.

Lyle Meeres lived in various parts of Alberta and Saskatchewan. At three different times he lived in Red Deer, which is his current home. A retired teacher, Lyle attended university in Edmonton where he obtained his degrees, and in Oregon. He writes essays, short stories, plays, and poetry.

Judith Anne Moody hails from Vancouver but loved living in Red Deer. She has published 'The Golden Eye' trilogy about a magical First Nations lad. She is now creating more contemporary tales of a bunch of country kids, from which these stories are taken. Judith is 73 with many kids and grandkids.

Patricia Mary O'Neill has been playing with words all her life, first in her imagination and much later by putting words to paper. She's had the good fortune to work as a writer (human interest, news and sports) for a small town newspaper. It was a great training ground to hone her skills.

Kathleen Piesse - "Telling stories" comes naturally to her. She has long practiced the process, for her own enjoyment, primarily through journaling and workshops. Membership in RDWI has encouraged her to expand her creativity, hence her entries in this Anthology. She is also working on an Historical Creative Non-fiction book/novel.

Carol Ritten Smith has published several short stories and two novels. You can find her work at Amazon.ca or Amazon.com under her name. She also enjoys pottery, sewing and other crafts. Her husband of forty-odd years, children and grandchildren fill her life with laughter. Her cup overflows.

Lorelei Roll - Attending country school in southern Alberta, a teacher encouraged her to write stories. Later, writing was limited to scientific papers while studying Horticulture and Botany. Now, writing creatively as a member of RDWI, she has a poem in this Anthology, and is working on a mystery novel, having a blind sleuth as protagonist.

Robert Willard Swann was born in Halifax, Nova Scotia in 1970; Educated at Millwood High School, Kjiputuk Community College, Nova Scotia Community College, and Henson College TYP. Grandiose Achievement: Blessed dependence and independence! Published writing: BIANS NEWS newsletters, Red Deer SDA newsletters, and "From Wayside and Woodland" poem. He resides in Central Alberta.

Nicole Tarry – Just your average 30-something with an overactive imagination; this extra has spilt out into writing down those crazy thoughts and ideas. The results are not always grand or epic, but they are her own. She's a happy yet slightly chaotic mom of two kids and a dog. She can also say that she's been married and living in Central Alberta for the last fifteen years. Even though she has taken up the pen with more seriousness in the past two years, she still considers herself fairly new to creative writing.

Alison Whittmire holds an interdisciplinary Master's degree and focuses her time on writing poetry and short essays, working for the Canadian Mental Health Association, and raising her young children. She believes strongly in the transformative power of words, and encourages everyone to find their voice and write their story.

Andrew Worzhak was inspired to write after considering how he might turn his experience as a Dungeon Master for Dungeons & Dragons into a career. He's been writing about characters that were inspired by the many fantasy novels he has read using experience as a DM to tell stories from unique perspectives.

Made in the USA
Charleston, SC
27 November 2016